"You asked me what I think about Noah Scott?" Ty laughs. "Oh, yeah," he says around his cig. "Your boyfriend's real fuckin' nice. What a cutie. I heart the fuck out of him. What a catch." I take the cigarette from my mouth and throw it at Ty. It doesn't come even close to hitting him. He snuffs it out with his boot. "Honestly? I want to smash his face in. Is that what you want to hear?" I cross my arms over my chest.

"I don't know, Ty. Jesus Christ, I wasn't asking you for dating advice."

"What were you asking me then?" he says and then sighs. I watch as Ty wraps this awesome self-control around himself. It's almost a physical change, very impressive, something I could never do. "Look, it doesn't matter. I'm mildly okay with this, alright? I mean, if you choose me because I tie you up in the bedroom and forbid you to see him, what good does that do me?" Ty pauses. "Though I'm not opposed to doing that if you're interested."

"Ty," I say, leveling a look on him. If he's going to freak out and run off, fuck some bitch behind my back, I want to know now.

"I want you to choose me for me," Ty says and my heart turns to slush in my chest. "I want you to say fuck Noah Scott and mean it. When you can do that, really do that, come tell me. It'll happen, I know it will."

Books by C.M. Stunich

The Seven Wicked Series
First
Second
Third
Fourth
Fifth
Sixth
Seventh

Houses Novels
The House of Gray and Graves
The House of Hands and Hearts and Hair
The House of Sticks and Bones

Indigo Lewis Novels
Indigo & Iris
Indigo & The Colonel
Indigo & Lynx

The Huntswomen Trilogy
The Feed
The Hunt
The Throne

Never say Never Trilogy
Tasting Never
Finding Never
Keeping Never

She Lies Twisted

Hell Inc.

DeadBorn

A Werewolf Christmas (A Short Story)

Broken Pasts

Fuck Valentine's Day

Never say Never.

C.M. STUNICH

SARIAN ROYAL

Finding Never
Copyright © C.M. Stunich

All rights reserved. Printed in the United States of America. No part of this book may be used or reproduced in any manner whatsoever without written permission except in the case of brief quotations embodied in critical articles or reviews. For information address Sarian Royal Indie Publishing, 1863 Pioneer Pkwy. E Ste. 203, Springfield, OR 97477-3907.
www.sarianroyal.com

ISBN-10: 1938623452 (pbk.)
ISBN-13: 978-1-938623-45-5 (pbk.)

Edited by Brandy Little of "Little Bee's Editing Services"
Cover art and design © Amanda Carroll and Sarian Royal
Optimus Princeps font © Manfred Klein
Conrad Veidt font © Bumbayo Font Fabrik

The characters and events portrayed in this book are fictitious. Any similarity to real persons, living or dead, businesses, or locales is coincidental and is not intended by the author.

*to those who thought they'd Never love again,
but found the strength to carry on.*

1

Ty and I are sitting on a dirty Greyhound bus with our hands tangled together between us. Neither of us is speaking, I think, because neither of us knows what to say. This is new territory for both of us and it's scary as hell. There's sweat collecting between our heated flesh, but I can't tell if it's mine or his or both because I can hardly breathe. I still barely understand what happened between us last night. All I know for sure is that making love and sex are two totally different things, and I can finally tell them apart.

I turn to Ty after too long of staring out the dirty window on my left and try to catch his attention by shaking his hand. It's not the one with the rings and bracelets, but I wish it was so that it would jingle. There's something decidedly cheerful about that sound. When he turns to face me, his dark eyes are contemplative and far away but happy, just a little bit happy. He likes me – loves me maybe – and it's putting this smirk on his face that tries to lift my spirit from the floor and shake it.

"If you gave notice at your apartment," I begin. "Where are you going to live?" Ty winks at me and pulls out a cigarette, pausing only because the old lady across the aisle from us is tapping him on the shoulder and gesturing angrily at the *No Smoking* sign that hangs crookedly at the front of the bus. Ty sighs and slips the cig back in his pocket. I think there's a time coming in the far off future where the two of us are going to have to quit. Not yet, not now though. I don't think I'll survive this trip if I quit now.

"Why, at the dorms of course!" Ty says as his hand moves from mine and finds a resting spot on my knee. It's only when he starts sliding it up my thigh that I stop him. I stare him straight in the eyes and try not to notice the girl in the front row who's been eyeballing him. He hasn't looked at her, not once. I don't think he even *sees* her. All Ty sees now is me.

"But you said you'd have nowhere to go?" I ask him and watch as his dimples fade and his smile becomes a little less happy, a little more melancholy. He nods and rubs at his chin with his other hand. His dark hair is still a bit damp, dripping tantalizing drops down the back of his neck that soak into the fabric of his already soggy T-shirt. We haven't been driving long, maybe an hour tops, and it's so fucking damp and humid in here that I've spent the whole ride with my window cracked, despite the rude stares from in front and the grumbles behind me.

"If you'd have turned me down, do you really think I would've stuck around? Gone to the same college? Fuck that, Never." I swallow hard and try to think up something to say. I don't know how to handle a situation like this. Love 'em and leave 'em, that was my previous policy. Now, here I am on a two thousand fucking mile drive with Ty McCabe who I don't know, not really. I feel him though, inside and out and everywhere and nowhere all at once. I am Ty McCabe and I'm not. He's me and he's not. It doesn't make any sense to me, but I know it's all true. I'm in love. I think. Things are bound to get twisted.

"What do you think Vanessa would say if she knew what we were doing?" I ask, thinking of our Sexual Obsession Group leader. "If she knew what we did … " I reach up and touch the chip that's still hanging from my ear. It was a proof of success and now it's a proof of failure, too. I start to take it off and stop only when Ty's long fingers wrap around my wrist.

"Vanessa would say, *Go get 'em girl,*" he tells me and pauses. "And she'd also say, *Don't you dare let her take that fucking earring off.*" I stare at him and know that he isn't telling me everything. His blue nose ring glints in the yucky fluorescent lighting as I slump back against the cracked window and try to enjoy the cool breeze against my neck.

"You talked to her, didn't you?" I ask him, and he smiles. I slap Ty's muscular arm *hard* and am satisfied at the cracking sound my gesture makes. His dimples are back though, so I can tell that he's in a good mood. I wish mine was as perky as his. But it can't be. It just can't because I'm on the road of no return. What I do here will define *everything* and I mean *everything* that will happen in my future. From Ty to my college career to my future job, all of it rides on this stupid trip. I know that and it's why I'm here. It's also why my past won't stop whispering dirty things to me, reminding me why I left and how my mother betrayed me and how my daddy's corpse is six fucking feet under, rotting in hell or heaven or floating through the river Styx … I don't know, and I don't claim to. All I know is that my family chose not to believe me, that they'd rather live with a murderer than face the truth.

I hate my mother.

"I called her after you left. I had a panic attack, Never. You can't just turn someone's world upside down and then leave."

"I can do whatever the hell I want," I tell him, but I do take his hand in mine and squeeze it tightly. I don't want Ty getting the wrong idea, getting off this bus and finding some other girl to bury his pain in. I close my eyes and try to fill my belly with air. He doesn't acknowledge my statement, just keeps talking which is fine with me. I could use a distraction from my thoughts. They're such a jumbled mess that I don't even know how to begin untangling them. *What am I doing on this goddamn bus? Why I am going back there? How do I even know they'll be happy to see me? What if I see that murderer in the flesh? What will I do? How will I react?*

"I told her that we made love, and she was supportive." I roll my eyes, but inside, I'm secretly happy that Vanessa knows. Despite my attitude in group, I look up to her, whether she knows it or not. "Although she did tell me that I was an asshole."

"You are an asshole," I tell him as I stare into his eyes. "You begged and pleaded until you got what you wanted. Feel better now?"

"No," he tells me as he leans across the seat and runs his hand through my hair, pulls my face to his and kisses the hell out of me. I can't even breathe; my lips are on fire and my heart has just exploded into a million pieces, been sucked out of me by Ty's breathe, the feel of his mouth against mine, the warmth of his body hovering so tantalizingly close. When he pulls back, he runs the knuckles of his ringed hand down my cheek. "I'm starving."

"For a sandwich?" I say, but I know that isn't even remotely what he's talking about.

"For you," he tells me, unperturbed by my attitude. See, Ty gets me. He gets that I'm fucked up and he knows that I know that he's just as screwed up, so we work together, him and me.

"This isn't going to be easy," I warn him, my breath brushing his lips and making him shiver.

"Fuck easy," Ty tells me and kisses me again. I keep my eyes open and watch the butterfly tattoos on the back of his hand. Somehow, even in this terrible light, they seem to sparkle with a bit of hope.

2

At the rest stop, I have my first panic attack. I stumble into the women's bathroom and lean against the wall with one hand while I gasp for breath and try to keep my head from spinning like crazy. *I'm going home ... I'm going home ... I'm going home ... It's been five years, and I'm going home.*

Women pass by and whisper but nobody stops to help me. I could be having a fucking heart attack and nobody cares. I force myself across the dirty tile floor and lean over the sink with my head hanging down and my hair kissing the wet porcelain. A watery reflection looks back up at me from the sink and shivers as I splash my hand into it. When I look up, I see Ty in the mirror behind me. He's standing at the entrance to the bathroom with a cigarette dangling from his lips.

"Want to talk about it?" he asks me as he moves aside for a group of giggling girls. They whisper and look him up and down as they pass. I want to say, *You have no idea what you're getting yourselves into. You can't handle a man like this.* But I don't. I just nod and follow Ty outside to a patch of grass under a small, sickly tree. It looks decidedly pissed off to have been planted next to the smelly restroom and I don't blame it a bit.

"This isn't about you," I tell Ty as I pull the cigarette from his mouth and take a drag. The smoke fills my lungs, clouds the severity of the situation from my frantic mind, just the way it always does. I sigh and watch the crackling cherry with pinpoint focus. "This is about my family."

"I figured as much," Ty says as he sits down and stretches out his long legs. They're encased in dark jeans, topped with a pair of black boots, no laces. Typical Ty. He looks incredible, perfect, edible, *dangerous*. I am playing with fire here and no matter what happened between us last night, I have to remember that. His shirt, after all, does say *Doesn't Play Well With Others*. Too true. "After all, how could anyone have a problem with me?" he asks with a smile. I smile back, but mine is tight. Ty nods and pulls out another cigarette, lights it, and blows smoke into the cool air.

"I don't know what I'm doing here." Ty's smile fades a bit as he takes the cigarette between two fingers. His bracelets jingle in the quiet space between here and there as he gestures for me to sit next to him. I fold my arms over my chest and wait. My nerves are stretched too taut to sit still, not when I know I have to get back on that bus. I start to pace.

"Sure you do," he tells me and I wonder when he got all of this control over himself. He seems so put together, not at all like the dark, tortured soul I know he is. Inside of him is a monster. I know that because I have the same one inside of me. Right now, it's telling me that my family doesn't give a shit whether I live or die, that they're happy I'm gone. *If you go back,* it says, *you'll only be digging your own grave. And Noah Scott? You were just an easy chance at a lay. He knew that then and he knows that now.*

"Shut up!" I shout as I clamp my hands over my ears. My cigarette flies from my mouth and topples end over end, hits the wet grass and fizzles out in the dew. Ty reaches over, grabs it and lights it again. When he hands it up to me, his dimples deepen with a heartfelt smile.

"You see that?" he asks, and I have no idea what he's referring to. "Even when you think the fire's been put out, you can always start it up again."

"What's that supposed to mean?" I say as I take it from his hands. I sound meaner than I want to and flop down next to Ty with the intention of holding his hand. Instead, he wraps his arm around my waist and pulls me to him, puts my head against his chest and cups it there with a handful of butterflies. I change the subject. "When you said I was yours … "

"I meant it," Ty says and that's it. We both stop talking.

3

Ty is an enigma to me.

He's still the wounded soul that I met at the bar, but he's also something different now. I can't quite put my finger on it, but when he looks at me, his eyes are full of color and life that attracts me like a moth to flames. I'm just going to have to do my best not to get burned. Ty could do that now, so easily that he could reduce me to a pile of ash without my even knowing it. I've given him this massive hold over me and my proverbial heart is beating in the palm of his hand, in his ringed, calloused hand.

"Tell me about your sisters again," Ty says sleepily. It's the middle of the day, but we're both exhausted. Granted, neither of us got much sleep last night. I smile. Frown. "I can't remember their names," he whispers into the crook of my shoulder and admittedly, I shiver. I'm not used to having a boy sleep next to me like this. His hair is so mussy and his face is so soft and vulnerable … "They were like the seven dwarves or something. Sleepy, Dopey, Horny … " I can't hold back a laugh as I pull at a clump of Ty's hair. "Ouch! Kidding, just kidding. Seriously though, tell me about them again." Ty pauses and I can feel a shift in the air. "Tell me about them and about Noah Scott." I swallow hard because I knew that was coming. As soon as I saw Ty at the train station, I knew it.

"In descending order," I start with a smile. "Beth, Never, Jade, Zella, India, Lettie, and Lorri." And then I stop talking because it's been five years. What if there are sisters that I don't know about? That don't know me? My throat closes up and I suddenly can't speak. Ty senses my shift in attitude and sits up so that he can look straight at me. He doesn't say a thing though, somehow sensing that there's nothing he can say.

"Hungry?" he asks and I nod. I'm starving in more ways than one. I'm just as hungry for Ty as I am for the sub that he's just pulled out of his bag. I stare at it, look at him and try to stop the world from spinning around me.

"Thanks," I say and my voice sounds very soft. It nearly gets stolen away in the rumble from the bus and the chatter of other passengers. Ty hears it though, and somehow I get this feeling that he will *always* hear it. A whisper, a scream, no matter what I say, Ty will hear me. I swallow and look down at the sandwich, unwrap the white paper covering and wonder how the hell he knew I liked pastrami and Swiss.

Finding Never - 11

"I just got you the same thing as me," Ty says with a slight smile and then he pauses and frowns, one hand still stuck in his backpack, eyes locked on me like he's just seen something that pisses him off. "Goddamn it, Never. Why didn't you tell me where you were going?" The change in subject is so abrupt that I find myself speechless. I pick up the sandwich, put it to my lips and chew. We both like Marlboro Reds, both eat pastrami and Swiss, and both have holes in our hearts big enough to swallow us whole. What the fuck? "If you'd have told me, I would've understood. I would've come."

"Good thing you got Swiss; I don't eat cheddar," I tell him as he starts in on his food. Like he cares about that. What he wants to know is why I tried to run, why I left him after everything we've been through together. Fortunately, he doesn't press his question. Maybe it's because he knows that I don't really have an answer for that. Because I got scared? Because I don't know what I'm doing here? Why I'm going? Why I even left?

"I fucking hate cheddar, too," Ty says instead, but he doesn't look at me. He stares down at his sandwich and then closes his eyes as he takes a bite, like he's savoring some five star fucking delicacy. I look at him and I wonder. I wonder how long he watched me stand there before he approached. I wonder how he knew I was going to be at the bus station. I wonder why he decided I was worth chasing down.

We sit in silence for awhile as the light outside the bus fades from yellow to pink, softens its way into night, into that quiet space that I could never stand. When I finish my sandwich, I hand the garbage back to Ty and watch as he stuffs it in his bag, leans back, and puts his arm around me. He turns his head so that his breath stirs my hair and sighs, nice and deep and long, one of those sighs that take everything that's swirling around inside of you and push it out.

"You've got all the cards now," Ty tells me, and I shiver because I was thinking the very same thing about him.

4

I fall asleep only because I'm exhausted. Ty and I didn't exactly get much sleep last night, and I'm so emotionally drained that I feel as if I've run a marathon. My hands are shaky again and my eyes can't seem to focus on anything. I lay with my head in Ty's lap, one tattooed hand in my hair and the other on my hip. Both feel good, warm, like they were meant to be there. At first, those two warm spots were what kept me awake, brought tears to my eyes and confused the hell out of me. As soon as I realized that Ty was not a dream, that he was not going to disintegrate, disappear, fade away while I was sleeping, I relaxed and drifted off.

Now the bus is rattling, traveling across rough ground, and I can hear the sound of gravel pinging off the bottom. It reminds me of so much of my mother's station wagon, of traveling in the backseat as a little girl, head on my sister's lap, eyes heavy with fatigue, that I sit up and find that I can't sit still.

"Nightmare?" Ty asks, eyes droopy but open. It's hard to sleep on this stupid bus, especially when I know we have a transfer coming up sometime soon. I don't remember where, but it's not too far off. I shake my head and my chip earring goes flying, smacking me in the cheek like it's punishing me for having sex with Ty. I clamp my hand over it and hold it against my skin.

"I can't sleep," I tell him as I yawn and and try to keep my eyes from lingering on his arms, on the sweeping curves of muscle, the swell of his powerful shoulders. "Talk to me." Ty takes this seriously and turns to face me, pulling one of his booted feet up onto the bench between us. He leans over and takes my hands in his. I rub my fingers over his rings, feeling the smooth cut of the blue gem beneath my skin. It feels real, but I don't know anything about jewelry, so I can't be sure. It's too pretty to be plastic though, like the sea without the sun, just a deep, dark piece of earth, cut and polished until it shines. I swallow hard and speak before Ty does. If he starts talking, he'll say something serious, try to get us into a real conversation, try to pick me apart and find out who I am inside. I know he'll do that because he's been doing that from day fucking one. "Where did you get all of these?" I ask as I count them. There are twelve. There have always been twelve. The number hasn't changed, even if the rings have. It's been the same since I met Ty McCabe in a bar and called him a whore, since he told me I wasn't worth it. I'm guessing he's changed his mind now. The way he's looking at me tells me that much, at least, is true. Ty McCabe thinks I'm worth something. How much is yet to be seen, but to me, he's worth everything. I just don't know that yet.

"These," he says as he squeezes my hand tightly but gently. "Were my mother's." I stare at the rings carefully, trying to memorize the pattern. I wonder if he ever takes them all off or if he leaves a set on always. I've never seen him without them, but then again, we haven't really spent all that much time together. It seems like a lot because every moment has been a mark on my soul, something to help bandage my bleeding wounds while it tears new ones and heals those, too. We certainly have a strange relationship. I've got to figure out exactly what it is, and if I'm going to keep it soon, just in case. I can't let Ty break me. If he does, then I'm done for. I will not survive.

He wears two on each finger of his right hand except for his ring finger. On this, he wears four, three silver bands and one gold with a red ruby in the center. I don't ask about the bracelets on his wrist. He changes these frequently; they're nearly always different. I think he wears those for fun and not out of any sentimental reason. The rings though, the rings are different.

"Were?" I ask, trying to fish for information. Ty has a past, just like I do, but unlike me, I don't think he's ready to face it. I hope I'm ready for this or if I'm being silly. I wonder briefly if, like Ty, I should keep a lid on all of this trouble. Still, if I do, I might boil over. I squeeze his hands back and try to find strength in them. Whatever he might think of himself, he has a lot of that. If he didn't, there's no way he could keep going the way he does. After all, he's the one that initiated change for us both. Not me.

"Yep," Ty says and then he closes up, just shuts down and pulls his hands away. He doesn't want to talk about it, and I can't force him. If I try, I'll drive a wedge between us that can never be removed. He sits back, slumps a little. He looks good like that, Ty does. He's got a perfect body, hard and solid, built for strength. I don't know how he got it or how he keeps it, but I like it. I swallow and look away.

"I don't know where we're going to stay," I admit, finally realizing that in my haste for emotional closure that I've forgotten all about practical concerns. I don't have any money; Ty doesn't have any money. But the thought of staying in my mother's house makes me shiver. If that ... that *thing* is there then I won't even consider it. I wonder if Beth ever got a place of her own and decide there's no way. She probably still lives in our family home, the one my mother inherited from my grandmother, the big rambling, Colonial that used to be the prettiest house on the block. If I hadn't run away, would I still be living there, too? Or would I have run off with Noah Scott? Would he have swept me off my feet like a knight in shining armor?

"We'll figure it out," he tells me, like it's that easy. Ty smiles and brushes a bit of hair from my face. "Never," he says quietly and I look up at him, wishing the fluorescent lights in the bus were off so that I could see the way his face looks in the moonlight. "Tell me about Noah Scott." I try not to sigh. Ty isn't going to let this go. He can't stop thinking about it. I should be asking myself why. He's worried about Noah Scott, but how come? I'm too fucking dense to see it for myself. Ty is scared he's going to lose me.

"What about him?" I say as I reach for a cigarette and then catch the eyes of the old lady across from us. She's glaring at me like I'm Satan himself. I put the cigarette between my lips and glare back at her. We're almost to our station, so I can wait, but I'm going to make her sweat along with me.

"I know you're going to see him," Ty tells me matter-of-factly, like he's accepted this but doesn't like it. "I know you need to see him, and I understand that. I just ... I want to know what you know. Tell me, Never, do you still love him?" Ty looks me in the face, pulls my eyes off the bitchy old lady and locks them in place. I try to focus on his eyebrow ring instead, but he won't let me. His gaze follows mine and sticks there like glue. I sigh, but keep my cig where it is. It's like a damn pacifier or something.

"I don't know," I answer honestly. I want to say *no,* but I can't. I loved Noah when I left and nothing but time has been there to put any damper on my feelings. I'm not the same girl I was when I left, and I can only assume he's not the same boy — man, I guess. I won't know until I see him, until our eyes meet, until he smiles that good ol' boy smile at me. Ty closes his eyes for a moment, but he doesn't look pissed, just afraid, oh so fucking afraid.

"What's he like? What's he do?" I shrug, but Ty isn't letting this go. He pokes me in the shoulder and his bracelets jingle. The old lady glares at his back, and I flip her off. She puffs out her chest indignantly and turns away.

"I haven't seen or heard from him in five years, Ty," I say, but he's already shaking his head.

"Maybe not," he tells me with a sad smile. "But you were stalking him online. I know you know. Tell me." I look down at my lap and think about the pretty pictures that Noah posts, pictures of dreamy, Midwest sunsets and crystal clear lakes, artful representations of dilapidated barns and rusted cars. But not of girls. He never posts pictures of girls.

"He's a student at the local college, a wannabe photographer and poet, and a blonde haired, blue eyed piece of Americana." My words do not give Noah Scott credit, but I know that they'll make Ty feel better, if only a little bit. "He's single, and his family is independently wealthy."

"Ah," Ty says softly. "My basic nightmare." I laugh and the cigarette falls from my mouth. Ty catches it just before it hits the ground.

The symbolism isn't lost on me.

5

Ty and I switch buses at the station, grabbing a quickie smoke next to the newspaper stands while the old lady files a formal complaint against me at the ticket counter. The representative gives her a five dollar credit, and she shuts up.

Our new bus is as dingy and dirty and unpleasant as the last, but at least Ty and I manage to grab one of the seats in the back. This limits the number of assholes I have to put up with and gives me windows to my left and behind me. Ty sits in the aisle again with his knees poking out. He's too tall to fit comfortably back here, but he never complains and he doesn't say a thing about me taking the window seat. I have a feeling that Ty is the kind of guy who would quietly give me the window seat on a plane ride, even if he'd never been. He's just like that.

I've got my phone in my hand now, and I am seriously considering calling Beth and telling her that I'm on my way, but I can't force myself to dial the number, to hear her voice desperate and frantic. If I tell her I'm coming then she'll be waiting, and the rest of this drive will be spent with my stomach in a knot and my lunch in my throat. Ty watches me quietly for awhile and finally reaches over, takes my phone from my hand and slips it in his backpack.

"Stop worrying," he tells me as we rattle along down the interstate, rocketing away from the ocean and school and my newfound friendship with Lacey. I was finally starting to get used to all of that, to enjoy it, and now here I am getting ready to throw a wrench in the works on a whim. "Everything will be alright." Ty scoots close to me and hugs me against his side, curling his fingers around my waist possessively as he eyes some rowdy guys in the front row with a look that says if he had the chance, he'd kick their smart mouthed little asses.

"Thanks for coming," I tell Ty because I can't imagine taking this trip without him. Honestly, if he hadn't caught up with me at the bus station, I might've turned around and gone right back, found him and thrown myself into his arms. I don't know what I was thinking, how I ever thought I could pull myself away from Ty McCabe. I glance out the window and notice the orange, rippling glow of the sun as it starts to burn away the night. *Two more days, and I'll be home. Two more days and I'll be standing on the precipice of disaster, ready to topple over and fall to my death. Please don't let this end me. I haven't even begun yet.* "But I can promise you this is going to be awkward." Ty shrugs, loose and easy. He doesn't care about that kind of stuff, not really. This is the same guy that walked into a full lecture hall and didn't notice the stares, that wears bracelets made for girls and still looks like the world's most masculine fucking badass.

"I wish I had something deep and inspirational to say to make you feel better, but ... " Ty winks at me and his eyebrow ring shimmers. "You're right. This is going to be awkward, and it's going to hurt like hell, and I'm sure you're going to wish a million times over that you never came, but Never," Ty turns to face me fully and tucks some of my hair behind my ear. "If you don't do this, you will always fucking wonder what might've been or what could be. That's no way to live. Even if this trip rips your heart from your chest and shakes you, even if it's the biggest mistake you've ever made, at least you won't be left wondering, and then we can move on. Together." Ty leans forward and kisses me. I part my lips and sigh at the heat of his mouth, the feel of his hand as it slides up my thigh, but all I can think about is that he said *we. We. We. We.* Ty McCabe and I are a 'we'? I wonder if maybe he's just being metaphorical and try not to read too deeply into it.

When he pulls away, he's got a dirty smile on his face.

"What?" I ask as he unzips his bag and pulls out a black sweatshirt. Ty shakes his head and his dark hair falls over his brow. I reach over and brush it away, trying my best not to get caught in his searing gaze. He licks his lips and my heart skips a beat.

"Your lips are like morphine," he tells me as I stare at him.

"What?"

"Haven't you ever heard that song by Kill Hannah?" he asks as he lays the sweatshirt across my lap. I wonder what he's doing because I'm sure as hell not cold. If possible, this bus is even hotter and more uncomfortable than the last. I try to push the fabric away but Ty doesn't let me. "*Lips Like Morphine?*" I haven't, but I get the gist of what he's trying to say and smile. "You could seriously kill somebody with those things." I chuckle. After all, it's impossible to have a tortured hottie like Ty say my lips are intoxicating and not grin like an idiot back at him.

"Thanks," I tell him as he puts his hand under the sweater and glides his fingers up my thigh. I don't catch on to what he's doing until his fingers brush my sweet spot through the jeans. I gasp and try to pass off the noise as a hiccup when the couple in front of us turns to stare. "What are you doing?" I whisper thinking that this feels too damn good to be real. After all those weeks of celibacy, Ty's fingers are like the greatest thing in the world, kissing and teasing the place he wooed with his body just a day earlier, just a day before when the world's simplest act became the most complicated, when I truly, honestly, and utterly fell in love with Ty. I clamp down on my thoughts and push them away. It's hard for me to have any logical brain activity with his fingers dancing a dirty jig across the clit.

"I'm entertaining you," he tells me as he leans closer and kisses my ear, my neck, my collarbone. The old lady from before is staring at us again, but I ignore her, convinced that she's jealous. How could she not be when she sees me with a guy as perfect as Mr. McCabe. *Wow. Wow. And double fucking wow. McCabe knows how to kiss. Okay. I can handle this.* "Did you know, in the olden days, that women who were having emotional problems could go to their doctors and have hysterical paroxysms. It was a cure all for their ills. That's what I'm going to give to you."

"A what?" I whisper, but my voice is barely a croak. Ty chuckles softly and scoots closer, one hand manipulating the core of me while the heat of his body draws me to him like a magnetic force. Ty has completely oozed into every crack of my psyche and sealed himself there. He's like a limb I can't live without, and I have no idea how I let him get that way. I'm supposed to keep people at arm's length, but with Ty, that isn't possible. It was never possible. As soon as I saw him in that bar, I was lost, gone, twisted up with his pain. Oh my fucking God, Ty McCabe is insane.

"A hysterical paroxysm," he repeats and the words, although unfamiliar, sound dirty coming from those wicked lips. "An orgasm."

I have to close my eyes to keep the noises back and pretend that nothing at all perverted is going on back here in the tail end of this bus. Old Lady is still glaring, and I hope she's not getting off to this or I'm going to kick her ass at the next station, gray hair or no.

"Ty," I say as calmly as I can which isn't all that calm because there's this tingle that's traveling from my clit up my spine and resting around my head like a halo. He ignores me and keeps nipping at the soft flesh between my neck and shoulder. I decide that he's not going to listen to words and push a bit of the sweater over his lap, so I can reach over and rub the bulge that's already appeared in his pants. This is a dangerous game that Ty and I are playing, but I have to say that at this moment, I'm thrilled to be one of the players.

He stops nibbling, presumably because he's as paralyzed by pleasure as I am, and leans his head against mine. We both close our eyes and pretend to be asleep, all the while flying closer and closer to that precipice that will take us over the edge.

When it's finally time to fall, I shudder in Ty's arms and he catches me, clutching my wrist and holding it still while I climax in the back of a bus full of strangers, drawn forward only by the gentle touch of his fingers through my jeans.

When I stop shaking, Ty pulls my fingers to his lips and kisses them a hundred times over. He doesn't let me finish him which I find incredibly ballsy. When I try to ask why, he says one thing and one thing only.

"I'm saving it all for you, baby."

6

The next two days are like some kind of fucked up fairytale consisting of dirty rest stops and stolen kisses, groping hands and moments of hand holding that remind me of the days I spent by the lake at home with Noah fucking Scott. I don't like to compare Ty to him, but I have to. For both their sakes. It's like this strange dream that I don't understand and don't want to wake up from. I mean, I went from fucking frat boys and guys whose only concerns were strippers, motorcycles and chicks, to making love to a dude with a blue nose ring and a heart that's black but only because it's been burnt and purified to ash. I don't know what to do with him or how to process what's going on between us, so I just live. For two days, I just am. I exist, and there's nothing else to it. *I think, therefore I am.* Descartes' most overused phrase is the one that fits me perfectly right now. I can't tell you what's real or what's actually happening, only that I'm me. That's it. It might not make sense, but it's true. And it's great. It's great until the bus drops Ty and I off at a dirty, weather worn bench in a town that closes down at six P.M. It's great until Ty picks up our bags (refusing to let me carry my own for some strange, male sense of courtesy that's somehow been bred into him) and we walk the mile or so down the road towards the house I grew up in.

I stand at the end of the driveway and my heart starts to pound like crazy. I'm glad Ty is holding my suitcase because my hands are shaking violently and my lungs are tight. I'm drowning. I'm drowning in memories and fear and anticipation. I turn around suddenly and stare Ty straight in the face. He looks nervous, too, but I don't know if it's because he feels bad for me or if it's just because he's in a new town, in a new state, with a bunch of people he doesn't know.

"I can't go in there," I whisper and my voice breaks. In that living room, my father took his last breath while the life was strangled out of him. In that very same living room, my family stood against me, protected a murderer with disbelief and lies, told me they hated me, wished with all their hearts that I was gone. I made their fucking dreams come true. I did exactly what they wanted, and I left. Why am I standing here? What am I doing? "Let's leave," I whisper to Ty as tears start to pour down my face. I can't move. I'm paralyzed.

"Never," he says as he puts our bags down and takes my chin in his hand. I move towards him like it's the most natural thing in the world, curl myself around his broad chest and breathe in the scent of cigarettes and some sort of spicy deodorant that smells like cinnamon. This scent becomes burned in my brain, forever there to remind me of Ty McCabe and the feel of his warm, muscular arms as they come around me and pull me close. "You can do this. You have to do this. This is your family. They're here, and you can't keep running. Memories are tricky mother fuckers, and they're fast, too. You can't escape them, baby. They'll always be there. You have to look 'em in the eye and be brave."

"What about you?" I snap, pulling back slightly. "I don't see you looking your demons in the face. All you do is fuck them." I stop myself before I can say anything else that I'll regret, and immediately try to apologize. Ty holds up a hand and stops me from speaking. His bracelets jingle in the quiet air, blend with the sound of crickets, a sound I've missed like crazy without even realizing it.

"Stop," he says and takes a deep breath. I can tell he's pissed at me, but I keep my mouth shut. "You're stressed out, okay, I get it. Relax." Ty McCabe looks up and over my shoulder at the white house with the gray shutters and the empty flower boxes, at the big front porch with the swing that hasn't changed a bit since I've left. The garden is a little sparser, a little less cared for, and there are different curtains in the windows, but otherwise, the house looks the same. I turn back around and study it with Ty in silence. None of the upstairs lights are on, but all of the downstairs ones are. People are home. My people. My family.

Headlights swing off the road and start towards us. I pray that they're headed down the road, to the Murphy's house, or what used to be the Murphy's house. It's the only other house down this way, or it was. I close my eyes, and I wait. Ty grabs our bags and starts to move out of the way, but when he sees that I'm frozen, he stops and stands there while tires roll across the dirt towards us and pause. Right behind me. They pause and I know without a doubt that there is someone in that car that I know. I think about running, about taking Ty's butterfly inked hand and disappearing through the fields, dancing away the night naked in a prairie, feeling his warm body caressing mine, diving into me, filling that aching hole of emptiness.

The car stops, the door opens, footsteps sound across the ground.

"Excuse me?" says the voice and then it stops, just cuts off like an engine. Silence reigns king for several moments. I know whose voice that is, but does she know me? Is that why she's stopped talking? Or maybe she's just seen Ty and gotten caught on how beautiful he is. "N-" Jade begins and then pauses, like she can't bear to say my name. "Never?" I don't answer; I can't. My hands are hanging by my sides, curled into tight fists while I struggle to breathe, to keep my head from cracking open and spilling my thoughts onto the ground in a tangled, bloody mess. "Never, is that you?" Jade's voice breaks a little, and I think I hear tears in it.

"I hate you, Never," Jade hisses at me. "From the bottom of my heart, I hate every last inch of you."

I whirl around in a cloud of dust, highlighted by Jade's headlights so that it looks like a cloud floating around my calves. I find my sister's hazel eyes in a strikingly familiar face, one that looks so much like mine that I draw a quick breath of surprise. There's so much hurt in Jade's eyes that they're nearly identical to my own. My pain mirrors her pain. How? Why? I wonder. What happened to her? Was it me? I take a step forward.

"Never," Jade whispers my name like it's the first word to a ballad, one that doesn't end well. "Never." And then we're both moving and our arms are going around one another and tears just fall, fall, fall. They hit the dirty ground and our sadness soaks into the Mississippi earth. For a long, long while neither of us speaks. There are no words for this moment, nothing in the English language that can encompass the emotions that I'm feeling. I think in colors for a second, in bright blues and hazy lavenders, grays that mimic the blue of the sky above the sea. And then I pull back and I look at a face that is too like mine for a half-sister. It's incredible. Jade and I are practically twins now. I touch her tears, wipe them away, cup her chin in my hand.

"I always knew you'd be prettier than me," I tell her and she laughs. It's a nervous laugh, but a laugh nonetheless, and I'm pleased with it. Her cheeks are covered with rouge and her lipstick is too dark, but I guess that nobody taught her how to put in on, so how can she be blamed? The only things my mother passed down to us were her looks and her love for men. I wonder how I'm going to react when I see her. I try to keep a smile on my face for Jade and touch her copper hair, wonder if I should stop dying mine, and drop my hand to my side.

"What are you doing here?" she asks me as she shoots a glance over at Ty. Her eyes travel his body, rate him, find something they like and flick back to my face. "Beth said you called, but I ... I didn't really believe it."

"I'm on winter break," I tell her, as if that explains everything. *Oh yeah, after five years I'm just home for break. Like that's gonna fly.* I don't know what else to say and neither does Jade.

"Um, let me get my car," she says, glancing over her shoulder at a beat-up old Toyota. "And I'll meet you on the porch?" I nod and step out of the way, wanting so much to talk to her but not knowing how. Jade glances over at Ty once more and smiles a coquettish smile that tells me that I'm in trouble. My whole family will want him, but not because he's Ty, not because he's a piece of tortured fucking art, but because he's mine. *Oh, fuck,* I think as I look at Ty, at the man who knows so much about me yet knows nothing at all. *I shouldn't have brought you, but I'm glad I did. I'm glad you chased me down and took my face between your beautiful hands.*

"Are you okay?" he whispers as Jade starts the car and inches it past us like we're made of glass. I nod, but I step into his arms again, let him hold me. He doesn't seem to have any problem doing that. I wonder how many freebies I'll get before he starts getting annoyed.

"I am now," I tell him honestly. "But I have a feeling this trip is going to kill me."

7

Ty picks up our bags and follows close behind me as we walk down the rest of the driveway and pause on the porch. Jade is standing there jingling her keys and biting her lip.

"Mom isn't home," she says and I cringe involuntarily. Jade sees this and stops shaking her keys around. Silence descends. "India's here, I think. Probably Lettie and Lorri. You haven't met Darla or Maple." My throat closes up, and I have to take several soothing breaths to open it back up. Ty's hand in mine doesn't hurt either.

"Who?"

"Darla is ... " Jade doesn't know how to phrase this which is a bad sign. "Darla is my little sister. Um, our little sister, I guess. She's only three, but ... " Jade glances over her shoulder. I can hear the TV blasting and India's perfect voice shouting. She sounds good even when she yells. She could've been something with that voice. Her songs could work their way into your heart and take over you and you'd never even know it. "Um, Maple is Beth's daughter." I swallow hard.

"Beth has a daughter?" Jade nods, but she doesn't speak. She's staring over my head at the glitter of lights in the distance, a small, sparkling reminder of the town I left behind. "A husband?" Jade shakes her head no. Of course not. Why did I even ask? I look over at Ty. He's playing with his lip ring, spinning it back and forth, sticking his tongue through the hole. My blood heats, and I have to look away. I'm in a stressful situation, and I'm thinking about sex. Figures. Or maybe it's just Ty. Maybe it's just him. I hope so. I touch my fingers to my chip earring and try to figure out how to ask my next question because I *have* to ask it. If I don't, and I see him, I'm done for. "Is – "

"No." Jade's response is sharp and rude. Her eyes darken and she turns around, reaches for the screen door and pulls it open with a creak. "He left a long time ago." Her voice softens and I see that her anger is not for me but for her biological dad, my mother's fiancee turned second husband, my daddy's killer. "Come in. I'm sure Lettie and Lorri will be happy to see you." She doesn't mention India.

Ty and I ascend the steps, and I realize that if he wasn't by my side that I'd have bolted as soon as I'd seen Jade, run right back to the bus station and gone home. I would've crawled between the covers in my dorm room and cried myself to sleep, waiting until I could go out and find a new guy to bury my sorrow in. I shake my head and know I can't go back to that.

"Jade!" India shouts from the direction of the living room. I'm standing with my back to the doorway, Ty's hand a captive in my hand, my heart pounding so loudly that I'm sure he can hear it. When he leans over and whispers in my ear, I jump.

"It's okay, Never," Ty says and presses a hot kiss to my earlobe. Shivers run up and down my spine and I feel my belly clench in anticipation of having Ty again because God help me, I want him so bad it hurts. Even now, even standing in this doorway to hell, I feel my body clench tightly, beg me to get to know Ty real good. It's never acted like this with another boy; *I've* never acted like this with another boy. Except for Noah Scott. Oh God and fuck and holy fuck, except for him.

"I need you to watch the girls until Beth gets home. I ... " India comes around the corner and sees Ty and me standing still as statues.

"Never is home," Jade says and bites her bottom lip. Tears prick her eyes again, and she turns away suddenly, flying up the staircase like she can't take the pain of seeing me. I hear her footsteps upstairs and the sound of a slamming door.

India is so fucking beautiful that I can't stand it. Last I saw her, she was only eleven years old, still just a kid, but now she's a woman with long, copper hair and a smile that will get her into too much trouble. She stares at me for a second and then she throws her head back and laughs. I laugh, too, but I don't know why and then she's running forward and throwing her arms around my neck like she used to do before I left. She squeezes me with real warmth, not an ounce of animosity or resentment in her touch. When she pulls away, she turns to Ty and smiles.

"Who's this?" she asks as tears roll down her cheeks and

she sniffles, making her look just a tad younger than her sixteen years. "Your boyfriend?" The question catches me off guard and I freeze with my eyes on Ty's face. He stops biting at his lip ring and smiles that heartbreakingly beautiful smile of his with the dimples and all.

"My name is Ty McCabe," he tells my sister as he takes her hand with his ringed one and shakes it. Her eyes travel from his jewelry to his butterfly tattoos to his broad shoulders and smiling face. She thinks he's pretty, that much I can tell, but she doesn't scope him out like Jade did. *India was always one of my favorites,* I think as she turns back to me and hugs me again.

"I feel like I'm dreaming," India says as she tilts her head to the side and touches the red streak in my hair. "This is beautiful. I love it." Before I can respond, my little sister Lettie walks in with a book in one hand, a notebook in the other. She's looking down at her notes and doesn't see me at first.

"India, can you help me with something?" she asks as she moves across the hardwood floor and I start to cry again. I don't know when I'm going to be able to stop. "This Christmas break homework is stupid. I don't get why we have to do it. It's a *break*, not a study session." She pauses and looks up, spots me and freezes like a deer caught in the headlights. Lorri skips in right behind her, sees me and stumbles for a moment, copper pigtails swinging with the momentum.

There's this terrible moment where I am absolutely positive that neither of them is going to remember me.

"Never!" they say in near perfect unison. The notebook goes flying and hits the staircase as Lettie and Lorri race forward and embrace me with the kind of innocence that's only found in children, the perfect, pure, love and honesty that gets bled out of the rest of us. I stand there and laugh while fat tears hit their pretty heads and India grins at me like a crazy person.

"Be right back," she says as she scoots reluctantly away. "I gotta check on the babies." I sniffle and gently move my little sisters back, so I can look into their eyes and thank the powers that be that they know who I am.

"I told you she'd come home," Lorri tells Lettie with an eye roll that seems inappropriate for her young age. Then again, my sisters and I have always been ornery. I suppose it just runs in the blood.

"Where's Zella?" I ask them, feeling my heart contract painfully. Zella's daddy was my daddy, and of all people, I had expected her to stand up for me, with me, against my mother's decision, but she didn't say a damn word, not one fucking word. If I'm going to make peace with my past, I have to see her.

"Zella moved to Texas," Lettie tells me as she turns to Ty and gives him a look that says she isn't buying what he's selling. "She's going to college in Austin." My heart drops.

"Oh," I say, and I try to keep my voice light. I don't want to ruin my reunion with the rest of the girls. I can always call Zella later or stop there on the way back to California. I smile at Lettie and Lorri and follow their gazes over to Ty. "Guys, this is my friend, Ty McCabe."

"Hey there," he says, bending down so that he's not towering over them. "Nice to meet you." Lettie looks at his ringed hand like it's diseased, but Lorri shakes it vigorously.

"Are you a rock star?" she asks him, and he laughs.

"No way," he tells her and he leans forward for a whisper. "Don't tell anyone, but I can barely carry a tune." Lorri chuckles as Ty leans back, and I can't help but hold back a smile. You know how they say you can judge a person's character by the way they treat little kids and animals? It's true. I can see in Ty's mannerisms how gentle he really is. The thought that anyone could hurt him, including me, pisses me off, and I hope to God that I never do.

"Where have you been?" Lettie asks, turning back to me with a frown on her adolescent face. At thirteen though, she's changing, entering that awkward phase between girl and woman. "I missed you, sister." I laugh again and take her into my arms for another hug. I can't tell her the truth, not yet. Maybe someday I'll take her to lunch and spill my side of the story. For now, I just ruffle her hair and come up with something explanatory but nondescript.

"I had to go to college," I tell her with a grin. "So I could become something kick ass awesome."

"Like?" Lettie inquires as I glance over at Ty. He's staring back at me like he's just as interested in my answer as she is. The weird part about all of this is that I have no fucking clue. What do I want to be when I grow up? I haven't the slightest friggin' idea. I feel like I've been living in a haze for five years and have finally just stepped out of it. Everything seems so much clearer now. I respond as best I can.

"Like someone who's in control, who's their own boss, who has a job that they can't wait to wake up for, and that keeps them up at night because they can't stop thinking about it." I don't know if a job like that even exists or I'm just spinning some serious grade A bullshit, but it sounds pretty and it satisfies my sister. For now.

"Hey there," India says as she comes back in with two copper haired girls on either hip. *Jesus Christ, we're like a family of clones. It's incredible. Guess those old Southern genes run strong and hard.* "Lookie who I've got. Never, this is Darla." India turns so that I can see the little girl's face. She's so cute I can't stand it. I step forward, but she buries her head in my sister's shoulder. I smile sadly, but know that I'll figure out some way to weasel into her affections, even if I have to buy her off. "Darla, that's your big sister, Never. Remember the pictures we looked at together?" Darla nods her head and sticks her thumb in her mouth. India shrugs and turns, so I can see the other girl. "And this is Beth's daughter, Maple. She's two and Darla is three." India juggles them expertly, making me certain that biologically those girls might be sister and niece to her, but as far as time spent and values learned, India is their pseudo-mother. *Goddamn you,* I curse Mom and Beth and wonder where the hell they are. Knowing my mom, she's probably dancing naked under the moon at some hippie-dippie fair, and Beth, well, she's probably slaving away at some useless, piece of crap, nowhere, dead end job. "They'll warm up eventually," India says as she turns and gestures at Ty and me with her chin. "I've gotta get them something to eat before all hell breaks loose."

She disappears into the kitchen with Lettie and Lorri at her heels and gives me a perfect, quiet moment with McCabe. I'm kind of glad because I've just gone into overload mode and feel like a robot about to short circuit. There is so much going on in my head right now that I need time to process things, organize them, figure out how to feel before Beth and my mom get here. They're going to be my two biggest obstacles in this marathon of pain, heartache, and healing, and I could use a water break before I get to them.

"How are you feeling?" Ty asks as he slides our suitcases to the side with his foot and steps closer to me. I have to really think about that before I answer him. Tears start to flow and I dash them away angrily. I hate crying. Hate, hate, hate it, and yet I can't seem to stop. I'm like a broken fucking faucet.

"Overwhelmed?" I say, but I'm not sure. Ty nods and tucks

my head under his chin. If nothing else, he understands. We're one in the same, Ty McCabe and I, and he'll always, always get me. Even if nobody else does.

8

The kitchen looks much the same now as it did when I left. There are dishes piled sky high in the sink, but not from lack of trying on either Beth's or India's parts (they were the only ones that ever did any chores around the house). It's just because there are so many people under one roof. One meal is all it takes. Sippy cups and plastic plates sit stacked neatly in the drying rack and rusted pots and pans hang from the ceiling interspersed with dried clumps of herbs that nobody uses but that make everything look homey and perfectly country. The refrigerator is littered with magnets and school photos, some that even date back to my days as a ballerina. Ty catches sight of one when he walks in and pauses, smiling as he examines the long lines of my arms and legs, the way the light caught on my copper bun that day. He fingers the edge of the photo and throws a glance my way that I pretend not to catch. I don't want to even think about the past right now. I can barely handle the present.

I watch as India sets Darla and Maple in matching purple booster chairs and wipes her hands on her jeans. She can't stop smiling at me, grinning from ear to ear like she's just won the lottery. I don't think I'm that cool, but I'm glad I can make her smile. After all the time we've lost, at least I can do that. Lettie and Lorri scramble up into the window seat together and lean forward like twins, elbows on their knees, eyes bright. I feel like some kind of miracle or something. It's kind of cute, but also a little bit scary. I can't mean so much to these girls or I might let them down, and I'll die before that happens.

"Beth is the assistant manager at the Clothing Case," India says proudly, naming the used clothing boutique that's existed downtown for as long as I can remember. They specialize in designer clothing that's already been worn and traded in for cash then resell it at a ridiculously overblown price. The girls at school were always obsessed with going there because that meant they could get the latest designer bullshit at half the price. Me, I stuck to Target. A tank top is a tank top, and a pair of holey jean shorts, well fuck me, I can cut up a pair of Salvation Army jeans and make a pair that cups my ass like a second skin.

"That's great, India," I say putting this ridiculous amount of pep in my voice. Ty's dark eyes slide over to me and he smirks. I ignore him, convinced that one day I'm going to end up meeting someone from his hazy, mysterious past and he's going to show me a side of himself that I've never seen. It'll be my turn then. "And … " I swallow. "Mom?" India sighs, and in her face, I see the same tired irritation that I always felt.

"She's on a date," she tells me as she pulls out a box of Cheerios and sets it on the counter. I scoot out one of the chairs on my side of the table and gesture for Ty to sit. He moves over and folds himself into it, a dark, sensual modern sexy against all of the light country décor. Somehow, it makes him seem even more beautiful. "And I'm supposed to watch the girls and set the table even though I have a ton of crap to do." India grabs a banana and cuts it into little circles before setting it on the table between Darla and Maple. Neither one touches it. They're both just staring at me with pretty hazel eyes that are so wide they look like marbles. India pauses, sighs, and turns around, holding her head to the side so that her hair hangs likes a copper sheet over her shoulder. "God, Never, I'm so glad you're here. I really … " She swallows and gets teary. "I really missed you."

"I missed you so much it nearly killed me," I admit, but I don't elaborate. She doesn't ask me to. Lettie and Lorri remain quiet, just watching, absorbing. I'm sure that once they get past their initial shock, they'll be all over me. I may not even be able to get rid of them. Not that I'd want to. Not in a million years. Whatever happens here now, tonight, tomorrow, next week, next *year*, I will not cut down the whole family tree because of a few bad apples. I make this vow in my head and smear it with the blood of my soul because I will *not* break it, no matter what Mom and Beth do, no matter what Zella says over the phone. Those are the three members of my family that I'm afraid might be the poisoned apple to my Snow White. I've got to be careful, oh so fucking careful.

"Beth should be home any minute. God, she's going to freak the fuck out when she sees you, Never. When you called, you should've seen her face. She was white as a sheet. I thought she might've seen a ghost." India heads to the fridge and pulls out some juice which she pours carefully into cups for Maple and Darla. I look around, wanting to help her but not feeling at home enough to touch anything. I might've grown up here, but I feel like a fucking stranger off the street. I glance over at Ty and am surprised that he looks relaxed and comfortable, not at all like this is weird for him. And it should be. It really should be. After all, this isn't his family, it's mine, and I'm ... what to him? A friend? A sponsor? A girl he made love to? A *girlfriend? No, can't be. Guys like Ty McCabe don't have girlfriends. They have fuck buddies and one night stands and ...* I stop myself and try to take a deep breath. Ty has changed; I have changed, and things are not always what they seem. He told me he loved me. How many girls he's said that to, I don't know, but I don't think it's many.

"Can I help with anything?" I ask finally as India pulls some rolls out of a plastic bag, throws them on a plate and sticks them in the microwave.

"Nah," she says, still smiling, still doing other people's chores with a smile on her face. "You're a guest. Sit down. It's alright, I got it." She pauses and glances over her shoulder at me. "Mom's supposed to be home soon with some of those rotisserie chickens from the store, you know, the precooked ones?" I really have no idea what she's talking about, so I shrug and sit down in the chair next to Ty. As soon as he gets the chance, he takes my hand and rubs his thumb over my knuckles, light, soothing, swoon worthy. I look down at it and then back up at him. I'm not used to this kind of stuff. I don't know how to have a boyfriend, a companion, even a friend. But I notice I don't pull away. I can't. I don't want to. *I just want a fucking cigarette.*

"So Mom's dating?" I ask, trying to fish for information,

but before India can answer, Jade walks in with the skankiest fucking dress I have seen on a girl, myself included. It's zebra print and oh so short with fishnet tights and a pair of leather high heeled boots. My eyes immediately snap over to Ty which is so dumb because really, would he check out my sister? He looks, but he doesn't think she looks very good. I can see in his eyes that he actually feels sorry for her. Did he feel sorry for me that first night he saw me in my skintight, red dress? But no ... His eyes swept me like I was a midnight snack, and he did hit on me, until I refused to go dancing with him. I wonder briefly what might've happened if I had. Would things have worked out as well? Would they be the same? I shake my head of what-ifs, and pull myself back to the present.

"Um, I'm glad you're here," she says as she slowly lets her eyes shift over to Ty's face, his body, his ... I clear my throat and she looks back up at me.

"You're not going out, are you?" Lettie asks, voice desperate. I can tell from her panicked face that this is something that's happened before. Jade shrugs and puts her hands on her lower back as she tries not to look awkward in her too tall boots. "But Never's home!" Lettie shouts, getting real angry, real fast. "You can't go now!"

"Go where?" I ask, suddenly feeling protective of the little sister I left behind. *The one that hates me,* my mind whispers. I ignore it.

"Just to a club," Jade says softly, voice barely a whisper. Maple starts to cry, and India's forced to pick her up and bounce her around on her hip. "I like to dance."

"Last I left, the only club in town was the Naughty Bunny, Jade. That's a fucking strip club." Jade's nostrils flare with anger and her eyes flash. I watch as her hands curl into fists and all of that repressed anger and hatred, it all comes pouring out of her and straight at me. I always knew, still know, that it's not all my fault, but Jade has relegated me to her emotional punching bag. Being gone didn't change that. She still hates me.

"Like you fucking care, Never. You ran out on us, so don't try and act like a big sister now, babe. That time has come and gone." Jade starts to turn away, but Ty grabs her wrist with his ringed hand. His bracelets tinkle merrily and everyone stops talking. Even Maple stops crying. Jade freezes and a pale, pink blush colors her cheeks. I can tell by the way her lip trembles and her eyes water that she's not used to being touched by guys. Maybe she hangs out at the strip club, maybe even dances, but she doesn't let men touch her or she hasn't yet. Jade might look like a whore, but I can tell with every instinct I have that she's a virgin.

"Listen," Ty says in this no-nonsense sort of a voice. It's compelling enough that even *I* kind of listen to it. Or maybe Ty just has a way with women. Doesn't matter anyway. I can tell he senses that Jade is on the same path that we've both traveled and barely survived. He's trying to help my sister, not for me or even for his conscious, he's trying to help my sister because deep down, underneath the tattoos and the cigarettes and the sleeping around, Ty is a good person. I suddenly feel jittery and my hands start to shake. "I know you don't know me, and you probably want to tell me to get my fucking hand off of you," Ty begins, and all I can think is, *Yeah, freaking right. Jade is practically eye fucking you. It's annoying, but God, she's my little sister and I don't care if she memorizes the curve of your ass, I just don't want her to end up broken like me.* "But there are stupid decisions and then there are fucking off the chart ridiculous ones. Jade, right?" Ty asks, and my sister nods, unable to find her tongue in the face of Ty's electrifying aura. "Don't make a decision today that you'll regret tomorrow." Ty drops her hand and it falls to her side like a dead weight. He turns back towards the table and smiles at Darla who won't eat any banana and reaches out, takes a slice between his calloused fingers and eats it. Almost immediately, the sister I didn't know I had until five minutes ago, reaches out and eats one, too.

"I like bananas," she tells him confidently and he grins, dimples deep and dark in that perfect fucking face. A sigh escapes my throat and I catch several curious looks from my sisters.

Luckily, Ty is too busy making faces at Maple who's laughing and pointing at his lip ring and saying, "Jewel, jewel."

"Beth's home!" Lorri shouts, peeping out the lacy curtains with a grin. Jade crosses her arms over her chest and looks embarrassed. When Beth sees her in it, she's going to get trashed. That is, if my sister hasn't changed a whole lot since I left. "Yay! Yay! Beth's going to be so happy, Never! She said you were the only line on her bucket list." The smile falls from my face, and I suddenly can't catch my breath. Memories flash like lightning before my eyes as I crouch over and try not to throw up.

Beth cracks me hard across the cheek. "Don't be selfish, Never," she snarls, pretty face not so pretty anymore. "Grow up. Don't you want Mom to be happy? Dad is dead, and he's never coming back, so get over it."

"Get her, get her," Lettie is saying to Lorri, pushing her forward as the two of them scramble to get out of the kitchen. My head spins and my stomach knots in a hundred places. My heart feels so fragile in that moment that I'm afraid it could shatter like glass, get stuck in my soul and bleed me to death. And then I hear Ty's voice, feel his hands sliding across the small of my back. My chair slides closer to his.

"It's okay, Nev," he whispers as he presses a gentle kiss to my cheek. In that moment, Ty really, truly falls head over fucking heels for me. Maybe it's the crying or the raw emotions or finally having a light shown on my fucking past, but Ty McCabe really, truly gets himself in so deep there that he can't ever get back out again. Nobody kisses like that if they're not in love. I know that somehow, but I don't. Maybe I don't want to, not yet. Not until I know for certain what's going to happen in this little town, in this little piece of nowhere, this nothing that means everything.

I hear Beth before I see her.

"This better not be a joke, Lorri, because it isn't funny." Footsteps, heels I think, move from the front door and pause at the entry to the kitchen. Ty turns around first and stands up.

"Hi there," he says, voice casual but firm. *He's afraid she's going to hurt you again. He wants to protect you. Ty wants to protect you, Never.* "My name is Ty McCabe, and I'm here with Never." He doesn't specify our relationship, doesn't define it. I like that about him. He doesn't want to corner me into a position, a title, Ty just wants me to be me. He always has. "You must be Beth." I hear his bracelets jingle, and I assume they're shaking hands, but I don't turn around, not yet. I have to get some oxygen in my lungs before I pass out.

"Never." Beth's voice is like a whisper on the wind, a tiny slice of air, a cluster of syllables. "Never." Harder this time, more emotion. "Never, I'm so sorry." And then Beth is sobbing and my chair is flying out from under me. I spin around, step past Lettie and Lorri and find myself in my big sister's arms. Her hand strokes back my hair while she rocks us back and forth like she used to do when I was little. She's wearing a pretty cream colored sweater dress and her hair is short and cut into a cute, little bob. I remain the only Regali to have dyed my hair. Beth pulls back and looks at me with big, round eyes jiggling with tears. Her lipstick is smeared across her teeth from biting at her lips nervously. She dashes her arm across her face.

"You had a baby," is the only thing I can say as I cry. Again. It's getting old and my eyes hurt, but I'm not through yet. This has to happen, I have to bleed this pain from my body or else it will poison me. Whoever says that crying is weak is obviously just a fucked up individual. It takes all of my strength to stand here and cry, to admit to myself that yes, I am sad, and yes, that is o-fucking-kay.

"I did!" Beth says, but that's all she can say because she's so busy squeezing the life out of me. "And I took a thousand pictures so you could follow every painful step." I laugh as Beth takes my face between her hands and looks me in the eyes. "I knew you'd come back," she whispers. "And I am sorry. I am so, so sorry." I take a huge breath, pull Beth's perfume into my lungs and say the words I have to say, the ones that have been sitting inside of me all along, the ones that were so angry to be there that they convinced me to do things I shouldn't do. I let the little monsters out, and I am more than happy to be rid of them.

"I forgive you."

I *feel* Ty smile behind me, don't ask how. I just know that he's standing there and that he's proud. I step back and feel like I should say something to Beth about him, like it's weird if I don't. She sees me step back and her eyes move to Ty's face. She looks at him and I can see what she's thinking. *This man is no good for my sister. This is the kind of guy that lies, that cheats on you when your back is turned, that's hot as hell in the bedroom, that's like fire to your ice, but who will melt you the first chance he gets.* I forgive her her judgments because I used to have them, too, but I know – or at least I think – that Ty isn't that way anymore. He's changed me, and I've changed him.

"Beth," I begin just as I hear tires on the driveway. It's my other demon. My big one. "This is … " I hold out my hand to indicate Ty in all his dark, twisted glory. "This is my … this is my Ty." Beth smiles.

"Nice to meet you, Ty," she finally says as Lettie grabs my arm and drags me back into the kitchen talking about rolls she made with India and how fluffy they are. Lorri is talking, too, and Darla is yelling, and there's just chaos everywhere. I'm not used to it, not anymore. There was once upon a time where I couldn't sleep without this noise all around me, this wild chaos, this mix of souls brushing against one another for the briefest of moments, but then I moved away and all I knew was loneliness. I knew how to connect my body with somebody else's, but I forgot about the rest of it. Slowly, oh so slowly, I start to remember.

"Help me through this?" I whisper to Ty, not realizing how much I need him in that moment. He presses the warm heat of his body against my back and bites my ear, just a quick nip before my sisters see, just a touch that paralyzes my whole being and gives me goose bumps.

"You've got me as long as you need me."

9

Beth herds me and Ty into the kitchen and sits us down, afraid of my mother's reaction. Because she's so emotional, because she's so happy to see me, Beth thinks that my mother will be, too. She highly overestimates the woman.

My mother walks in with a pair of grocery bags in either hand. She doesn't see me at first. There are so many people in the kitchen that I can't really blame her. A sea of familiar faces surrounds me, girls and women with the same small, pointy noses, curved lips, and hazel eyes. We've all come from her, were born from her womb, and yet, we mean less to her than she means to herself. I don't think that's the way the world's supposed to work. How are you supposed to put yourself out there when there's nobody standing behind you? I thought the purpose of having parents was so that there was always someone there that loved you for you. Guess I was wrong.

"Sorry, I'm late," she says as my sister, Beth, takes the bags from her hands with a sloppy smile and eyes full of tears. My mother pauses and looks her in the face for a long moment. She's wearing a halter top without a bra, a full, Gypsy skirt, and a pair of dangling earrings that swing like purple pendulums when she turns her head to face me. Time ceases to flow for a moment, breaks around us like waves around rocks. Her copper curls are scooped up like ice cream on her head, still just as pretty and shimmery as they were when I left, but her face is lined with pain and worry. This gives me hope for a brief moment, makes me think that something will change between us, that she'll be the mother I always wanted but never had. My heart starts to pump and I have to reach under the table and grab Ty's hand with an iron grip. It's slick and sweaty, almost as wet as mine with worry and fear.

"Mom." It's one, simple word, one that gets Beth sobbing again and makes India smile. Jade remains emotionless, and the younger girls, too wound up to keep this tense silent, start to talk all at once. I don't hear any of them. I keep my gaze locked on my mother's and I smile through the tears that just won't stop. *I'm home, Mom,* I think at her. *I'm finally home.* I feel my heart healing, just a bit, just a tiny scab that covers some of the pain. And then she speaks, and it all goes to hell.

"Oh, Never?" she says, like she saw me yesterday. "You're here for dinner?"

Beth's face falls and Jade scrunches up her nose. The little girls, except for Maple, stop talking. She's still babbling nonsensically at a pair of dolls she's got on the floor near the refrigerator. Ty looks over at me and I can feel him asking if I need anything with his eyes. He can sense that I've just been pushed even closer to the proverbial edge. I've stumbled so far that I'm teetering now. Nobody but Angelica Regali has this power over me. Nobody except Ty McCabe. But then, he's sitting quietly by my side watching my life unfold like some sort of origami nightmare while my mother pretends that this is not the first time she's seen me in five fucking years.

"Really?" I whisper, my voice hardly audible over Maple's baby talk. "That's all you have to say to me?" I sound angry, furious. I can't hold my emotions back, not anymore. Holding back has gotten me where I am today. It's a miracle that I'm not halfway to the grave, riddled with disease, and broken in two. *Because of Ty.* I start to shake again when Angelica rolls her eyes to the ceiling and puts her hand on her hip. She sighs deeply, like she just can't be friggin' bothered.

"Never, you disappeared for five years without even the courtesy of a phone call. It's been a long while since I cried over you, honey. What do you want me to say? What was I supposed to do? Chase after you?"

"Well, for starters," I say as I drop Ty's hand and rise to my feet. My chair squeaks across the linoleum floor. Maple starts to cry. "You could say 'Welcome home,' or 'It's nice to see you'. How about something like that?"

"Oh for Goddess' sake, Never Fontaine Regali. I'm glad to see you, but I'm not going to throw myself at your feet."

"It's Never Ross," I whisper. "Never Nicholas Ross." My mother freezes and for once in her selfish, miserable life doesn't know what to say. Regali is her last name; Fontaine was her choice for a middle name. Nicholas Ross was my father's name and now legally, it's mine, too.

"I see." This is all she says. Rage bubbles hot and fierce

inside of me until I'm seeing red and purple and black swirls in front of my eyes, spinning away to nothing. Ty stands up and puts a hand on my shoulder, but it's too late, I've already snapped. I swing my arm at the basket of rolls India put on the table. They fly off the linoleum top and smash into the counter. The red and white checkered napkin flutters to the floor and lands on top of the bread.

Nobody speaks, but Maple continues to cry. Beth moves over to her and picks her up, tucks her tiny head beneath her chin and coos soothing words at her. I hope Beth is a better mother than Angelica because otherwise, I don't envy Maple the life she's going to have.

"Never," India begins, but I hold up a hand.

"Maybe this was a mistake," I whisper, wondering why the hell I came back here. To tie up loose ends? Really? I thought it would be that easy, that I could walk in here and be part of the family again? To be honest, it looks like they've done just fine without me, learned to function without Never, adapted to life without her. Do they really need me back? Do they really *want* me back? I move towards the door and Ty follows.

"Please don't go," Beth calls after me, tears thick in her voice. She, at least, seems like she wants to make up with me. I pause with the screen door against my hand and look over at her. She's begging me with her eyes to stay. They're all bloodshot and red and puffy making her seem less like a Barbie doll and more like a person. That's the Beth I knew and loved. I smile, but it leaves a bitter taste in my mouth.

"I'll be back," I say as I move outside with Ty at my heels. India follows not too far behind and stands next to Ty while I stare up at the moon and try to get my head to stop spinning.

"Never," McCabe whispers and I have to close my eyes against his words because his voice is so perfect that I can't stand it. I want to turn around and throw my arms around his neck, cry into his chest, and let him hold me, but I can't do that. Not yet. I've seen everyone I need to see. Except one. Except for Noah fucking Scott. As soon as I lay eyes on him, speak to him, I'll know what to do, if coming here was right or wrong.

"Do you have a car I can borrow?" I ask India thinking that it's really weird that I can even ask that question. When I left, she was eleven. Now she's sixteen. *Holy shit, time really does fly, doesn't it?*

"Um, yeah," she says, voice so soft and perfect but not weak, never weak. I spin to face her and smile, this time without all of that bitterness. Her dad was a wandering musician, a guy who wore tight pants, cussed a lot, and sang ballads that could break your heart. My mother let them, but at least she got India. I kiss my sister's forehead and look over at Ty. He looks fucking perfect in the Midwest moonlight. It's different here, more pure somehow. I don't know why; it just is. I study his face with the glimmering piercings, his dark brown eyes, his colorful tattoos, and hold out my hand for a cigarette. India, maybe sensing that we need a moment alone, says, "I'll go get the keys," and disappears inside for a moment.

Ty digs around in his back pocket, finds the box of Djarum Blacks and hands one to me.

"I think this counts as a special occasion," he says softly, and I find that I can't agree more. Whether it's good or bad or beautiful or horrid, it's certainly special. How many family reunions will I have in my life? Hopefully this is the last. Hopefully I can find the strength to embrace them now or walk away forever. That's the plan anyway. Ty lights his cigarette first and leans down, pressing the cherry against mine. I inhale deeply and imagine that I'm inhaling more than the scent of cloves and tobacco, that I'm inhaling bits of Ty McCabe into my lungs, taking him deeper into me than I've ever accepted anyone else. I do this because I know the next thing that I'm going to say will break his heart. I can only hope that he understands.

"Here are the keys," India says, stepping out on the porch and giving us both looks that say she's gotten the full anti-smoking propaganda that they spew in classrooms nowadays. I think to myself that she's a good girl and better off for it, but I don't put my cigarette down. "It's the old Ford by the barn. Sometimes it takes awhile to turn over, but it's a good truck." I hold out my hands and tilt my head upwards so that I blow smoke towards the stars and not at India's face. The little monster is back, thanks to Mom, and it wants me to, wants to push her back and ask why she's smiling so big and looking at me like I'm so cool she can't even stand it. I don't want her to look at me that way because it means she looks up to me. Nobody should look up to me, not now, not ever.

"Look after Ty for me while I'm gone," I say, dropping my chin and smiling at her. I let the cigarette dangle from my lips while I dig around my pockets and find my phone. "Let's trade numbers in case you need me."

"Where are you going?" Ty asks as he grabs his cigarette between two fingers and crosses his arms over chest. His arm muscles tense, but his hand hangs limply while smoke curls through his nose ring and kisses his hair. I smile at India and wait for her to plug her number into my phone before I speak. Again, she somehow senses that Ty and I need another moment and bows back into the house. She isn't far away though, none of them are. I can hear them arguing about me in the kitchen as Ty raises his dark brows at me. "Well?" he asks, and I have to swallow three times before I can say what I need to say. "What's so fucking important that you can't take me with you?"

I drop my cigarette to the porch, amongst a heap of others and let it fizzle out on its own. When I raise my head, my eyes are closed because I can't look at Ty's face while I say this. I open my mouth three times and stop before I can ever utter the first syllable. *Why am I so fucking scared? What is wrong with me? Am I afraid of losing Ty? Do I even have enough of a hold on him to lose him?*

"Come on, baby," he says with a sigh, and I smile slightly because I've never liked hearing a guy say that before. *Baby.* It's always come across as something condescending, some stupid fucking pet phrase that makes them feel better about fucking me and walking off, like somehow calling me a nice name makes all the difference. Not with Ty. That's not at all how it is with him. "If you're going to walk away and leave me alone with a bunch of people *you* don't even know, you at least owe me an explanation. Where are you going?" My eyes pop open and my lips part; the words fall away like the last leaves in winter.

"To see Noah Scott."

10

Ty blinks so slowly that for a second I think that something's wrong with me, that I'm not seeing the world in real time anymore.

"Fuck."

That's all he says, just that. He's understandably upset by my statement, but he doesn't yell or throw something, he just stands there and looks at me like I'm some sort of treasure he's just found and doesn't want to let go of. His look makes me uncomfortable, and I glance away.

"I know it's weird to leave you here, but I … I just need to get away from my mom for a second, and I need to see Noah, and I want to take you with me, but I … "

"But you're still in love with him?" Ty says, lips tight, cigarette falling away into ash, hitting the toe of his boot.

"I don't know … "

"Fucking A, Never. If you are just say it." Ty is angry. I get that. I do, but what can I say? Maybe cramming all of this shit into one night is a mistake, but I know that there's no way I'm sitting still right now, not with all this wild, crazy energy inside of me. I have to see Noah Scott and complete the cycle, so I can process things. It's the only way. I asked for Ty's help with my family, and in a way, I'm asking for it again. I need him to stay here, to let me do this on my own.

"You could wait in the car … "

"Never, no." Ty steps forward aggressively, and I meet his gaze with my own. His hand wraps in my hair and he pulls my face roughly to his, kissing me hard, marking me with his teeth, his tongue, his heat. I groan into his mouth, grab onto his lip ring and suck it into my mouth. He's the one that pulls away first, that drags his face from mine on the edge of a moan. I'm vaguely aware that India is watching from the screen door, but I can't help myself. Ty McCabe is the world's most tantalizing treat. "I am not going to go. I'm going to sit here with your weird fucking family who don't know me and think I'm some kind of punk rocker turned heroine addict while you dance the night away with Noah mother fucking Scott. And I'm going to do that because I love you."

"Ty, stop."

"No." Ty grabs my arms firmly but not roughly. He makes me look at him, and I can see in his face that he isn't going to take any of my shit, not right now. "No, if you're going to do this, you're at least going to listen to me. I love you, Never.

You might think I'm blowing smoke up your ass or trying to get into your pants or whatever, but listen to me. I have been with a lot of women." I try to turn away, but Ty grabs my chin and stops me. "I have been with a lot of women," he repeats, making my blood boil hot and angry. *And you've been with a lot of men. Get over it.* "But none of them, not a single fucking one, has made me feel the way you do." Ty puts his ringed hand over his chest. "When I'm with you, Never, I feel like somebody who can do something, who means something, okay? So, listen, I don't know how you're going to find Noah Scott or if he already knows you're coming or hell, if you've been having cybersex with him for five years, and I don't give a shit. What I do know is that I love you, and that I want you to find yourself and come back to me. You do what you need to do, Never, and I'll be here waiting for you when you're done." Ty releases me and steps back, digs out another cigarette and lights it with shaking hands. I'm standing there speechless and angry with myself because I know that even though Ty just gave me a piece of his dark, bloody, beating heart, that I'm going to get in that car and drive away. I'm going to drive away, but I vow to myself that I'm just going to see Noah and come right back.

After all, how could I not when I have a man like Ty McCabe waiting for me?

11

I go to the Dairy Queen because it's the only place in town that sees any action after nine o'clock. Besides, I've done some cyber stalking on my phone and see that Noah's posted something about the milkshakes being good tonight. *Would be better,* he writes, *if I had some company to share one with.*

I pull into the gravel parking lot and try not to stare at the faces there. If I do, I'm bound to find one that I recognize and I don't think I can handle anymore than this right now.

You do what you need to do, Never, and I'll be here waiting for you when you're done.

I squeeze my eyes closed against tears and smoke a quick cigarette before getting out of the car.

Sometimes they leave and they don't come back; sometimes that perfect, little butterfly gets out of the jar and flies away, flickers like a bit of fire across the sky and disappears. If you love it, you'll let it go. That's what they always say, but they Never tell you how to deal with the pain of their leaving.

I remember Noah Scott leaving me with this not so cryptic message, and the days and weeks after that that I cried for him. Once, I even put my stuff in my car and started the drive back. I got halfway home before I panicked and turned back around, fled into the arms of a guy who knew all about motorcycles but nothing about girls with broken hearts. He was nice enough, but he was no Noah Scott.

At the door to the Dairy Queen, I catch sight of him sitting in a booth in the back corner and I get dizzy for a moment, stumble away and throw up in the scrubby bushes next to the dumpster. I'm nervous *and* I feel sick. I chalk it up to the stupid, fucking bus ride and smoke another cigarette. It's the best I can do considering I don't have any mints or gum with me. *Great. Your reunion with Noah Scott will smell like puke and desperation, Never. Isn't that the perfect fairytale reunion you always wanted?*

My phone rings and I check quickly to see who it is, thinking that maybe Noah saw me and is calling to say something cute like, *"Hey you, I caught you. Coming in?"* but the call isn't from Noah, it's from Ty. I've been gone fifteen minutes and he's already calling me. Good sign or bad.

"Hey," I say, trying to keep my voice perky but not too perky. I don't want Ty to think I'm having a super good time with Noah. If he thinks that, I don't know what he'll do. I know Ty is the type of guy that gets spooked easily because

I'm the type of girl that gets spooked easily, and I know that if he was out with an old girlfriend, I'd be stalking him like a crazy person. I have *never, never* felt this way about a man before, and it's confusing as hell. I think of the tears I shed while we were making love and have to close my eyes to process all of the emotions that I'm feeling. We might be more than two thousand miles away from the scene of the crime, but the emotions have trailed along behind us. The distance we've traveled is tricky; it convinces us that it's been awhile, that Ty and I have been some kind of unit for ages, but that's not true at all. Ty and I are a seed that's just been planted, waiting to bloom, wanting to bloom but not knowing how. It's been four days since we made love. Four. Days. That isn't long at all. Ty doesn't respond, but I hear him breathing. "Hello?" I ask, wondering if there's something wrong.

"Fuck," he says, and I smile because that's such a Ty thing to say. "Just fuck Never. I lied. I'm not okay with this."

"Why?" I ask him as I steal a glance over my shoulder. The door to the Dairy Queen opens and a group of girls walk out dressed in tight blue jeans and skimpy tank tops that can't possibly be keeping them warm in the nippy winter air. I ignore them, glad that I don't recognize any faces there. "Because I'm yours?" I ask him when he doesn't respond right away.

"Exactly," Ty says and then sighs. "Never, I don't know much about this whole girlfriend thing, but I do know that I don't like you hanging out with other guys." I freeze and the air escapes my lungs in a whoosh. Did he just say *girlfriend?* Did Ty McCabe just say that word? Why? How? I move the phone away from my ear and take a deep breath before I speak.

"I don't know what to say," I admit.

"You don't have to say anything," he tells me with a sigh

that matches my own. "And you don't have to do anything different. I'm not the kind of guy that wants to chain chicks up in his basement or pound my chest like some kind of testosterone fueled alpha male, but I … " Ty pauses and the silence is poignant and important, a memory that I mark for remembrance. I don't know why, it's just one of those historical moments in life that you don't appreciate until they're over.

"But?" I prompt and Ty laughs softly.

"But I want to drive over there and beat the shit out of Noah Scott." I laugh, too, and then there are tears in my eyes because all I really want to do is drive back to my mother's house and see Ty. I know in my heart that that isn't right. I *have* to see Noah Scott and find out. I'm not exactly sure what it is I'm finding, but I know I have to search anyway. When I find what I'm looking for, I'll know. "Just … don't do anything you'll regret, okay?" Ty says and then he hangs up. What he really means is, *Don't sleep with him.* I can read that message loud and clear. In fact, it might as well be written in blood against the moon's pale surface. And I'm not. I'm not going to sleep with Noah Scott, not when Ty is sitting on an old wooden porch smoking a cigarette and thinking of me and only me.

I stuff my phone back in my pocket, turn around, and head straight for the door of the Dairy Queen. My eyesight becomes focused to a narrow point in front of me, locked onto a blonde head and blue eyes, a face that's tanned from the sun and a smile as sweet as rain.

Noah Scott is reading a book and basking in the smell of grease and French fries and noise. He always liked noise. Noah Scott is a people person. He's sweet and he's kind and he knows things other people don't. Noah could put me on the straight and narrow, clean me up, change me, but then, Ty already has. Dirty boy Ty McCabe has done more for me than Noah Scott ever has. I pause next to the table and slide my nails down the pages of Noah's book so that he's forced to tear himself away from the words and look up at me.

One. Two. Three. Time trickles away from us as the smile I've plastered on my face starts to fade.

"*She Lies Twisted?*" I ask, inquiring after Noah's book. It's a dark title with a pain that matches my own. I have a coverless, wrinkled copy under my bed in the dorms. I've read it a hundred times sore and then I find Noah Scott with it wrapped in in his hands, and what am I supposed to think? He's staring at me like I'm a ghost, like he can't believe I'm standing there in the bright lights of the Dairy Queen with laughter a steady backdrop behind me.

"Never ... " Noah whispers before he drops the book, stands up and throws his arms around me. Noah Scott squeezes me tight, and I start to cry. Again. I guess I won't stop until I'm done bleeding all of my pain and hate and anger from my eyes. Once it's all gone, maybe then I can look at the people from my past with dry eyes and a true smile, one that's as real as the dimpled grin that Ty McCabe has. Noah hugs me so hard that I can barely breathe. He's warm and he smells good, like flowers or a spring brook or something. He's light and soft and the complete opposite of Ty.

After a moment, Noah steps back and looks at me with the slightest hint of tears in his pretty, blue eyes. He holds me at arm's length and just stares like he's the luckiest man in the world.

"I can't believe it's you," Noah whispers as he drops his arms to his sides and shakes his head.

"I got your text," I croak out as I lower my gaze to the floor. It's all I can say.

"Yeah?" Noah asks and then, "God, I've been missing you

like crazy." My head snaps up and my heart begins to thump. When Noah reaches out and touches my face, runs his thumb along my jaw, I know I'm in trouble.

I'm in love with Ty McCabe. I was once in love with Noah Scott.

Talk about a rock and a hard place.

12

"God, I just ... wow." Noah Scott runs his hand through his pretty blonde hair. It's so shiny and perfect, like he just stepped out of a shampoo commercial or something. "I don't know what to say," he admits as he looks me up and down and, apparently, approves of what he sees. "You're even more beautiful than I remember," he tells me, and I blush. I. Blush. Me. Never Ross, the whore from the Northwest, the girl with the broken heart, and the parade of faceless guys she doesn't remember. What the fuck?

"I ... " That's all I have. Just that one word. Just *I*.

"I can't believe you're here," he says as he steps back and holds his hands out, palms up, to indicate my person. Noah's blue eyes are sparkling, clear as glass, bright and happy and cheerful. I can see right through him, see that he's a good guy with a kind heart and fluffy, candy coated dreams. Noah Scott and Ty McCabe would not get along very well. "I have so many questions," he begins and then I see something interesting, a glimmer of dark pain. Noah Scott is very good at hiding it, but it's there, and it's all because of me. Shit. "I want to ask you a million things and tell you a million more, but I ... okay." Noah takes a deep breath and smiles. "Are you hungry?" he asks. "You look hungry. Let me get you something to eat, okay?"

"Okay." It takes me a whole lot of effort to speak that word. Noah grabs my hand and my fingers tingle just a bit, like I can see them being coated with fairy dust or something. *Noah. Noah Scott. My Noah. The guy who asked me out in the middle of a math test with a note, the guy who didn't think it was lame to kiss me in front of the whole school on Valentine's day, the guy who moved gently inside of me my first time, who kissed away my fears and showed me a brief glimpse of what love could be.* I start to panic. "Noah," I gasp, and he pauses to look back at me. His eyes are wide, like he needs to keep them open, so he can see me clearly, so that I won't flicker and disappear, some evanescent memory that fades at the touch of the sun, just a bit of moonlight. I choke on my own saliva and wrench my hand from his. "Just a second, just one second." I stumble to the bathroom and Noah follows. People are looking at us now and whispering. I think maybe they've just recognized me. I hit the girls' bathroom and step inside, closing and locking the door behind me. Luckily, it's not a set of stalls, just a single toilet that I have all to myself. I sit down on the floor and pull out my phone. I don't know who to call. Who do I have that I can rely on? That I can tell secrets to? I think frantically and decide there is only one person besides Ty McCabe that I'm not related to that might be able to help.

I call Lacey.

She picks up on the third ring and starts to talk.

"Hey Nev! I texted Ty to ask how you were taking things and he said you were with Noah. Is he still cute? Are you into him?"

"Lacey, stop," I say, and she does. She goes quiet, and she just listens. "Help me."

"Are you in trouble?" she asks, and her voice is fearful like it was the day at the convenience store, the day she thought some prick was going to force himself inside of her. The memory makes my vision go red, and I have to clamp down on my rage. Because Ty was there, he and I were able to save Lacey. She's okay, so there's no need for me to add even more emotions to the boiling pot I've already got on my stove.

"I think so," I say. And then, "No." I consider hanging up but can't. "I love Ty." Lacey doesn't speak, but I can hear her breathing. "I don't know about Noah Scott. I thought I could see his face and say *no,* but I can't. I can't. I just can't. I want to talk to him, find out where he's been and what he's doing, but most of all, I want to know how he feels about me. Is that normal?" I can seriously hear Lacey smiling on the other end of the line.

"Never, don't beat yourself up. Of course you want to see Noah. He was your first boyfriend, and let's face it, you didn't break up with him. You didn't fall out of love or have a fight or catch him cheating, so you're still connected in a way. You might always be connected. What you're going to have to do, and what I don't envy you for, is you're going to have to make a choice."

"A choice?" Lacey sighs, but I don't think it's at me. I think she's digging through her own life to give me this advice.

"You might love Ty, but you might also love Noah. That's okay. There's nothing wrong with that, but you can't have them both. They need all of you, and if you can't give it, you have to give one up. Pick one and be sure you're making the right decision because once you do, that's it. There's no going back, especially with Ty." Lacey pauses. "And Never?"

"Yeah?" I croak, not entirely convinced that calling her was the right idea.

"Please don't be an idiot." And then she hangs up on me. I stare at the screen and am tempted to crush it between my fingers and flush it down the toilet. Fuck. Fuck. Fuck.

"Never?" Noah is inquiring after me, as any proper gentleman should. Ty would've busted down the door with his big boots, cigarette in hand, and said, *What the fuck is wrong with you?* I smile. "Are you okay?" I stand up and straighten my sweatshirt. Oddly enough, it's actually Ty's sweatshirt, and it just happens to be the one he threw over my lap while he fingered me on the bus. Great. Perfect. Just what I need, reminders of Ty's skillful fingers while I'm with Noah. As if that isn't going to overcomplicate the already overcomplicated. I don't answer him, but I do turn around and open the door.

Noah smiles at me.

"Sorry," he says unnecessarily. "I just feel like if I take my eyes off you, that you'll disappear."

"What did you do?" I blurt too loudly in the middle of a freaking Dairy Queen. "What did you do when you woke up, and I was gone?" I take strange, shallow breaths as I ask this question, and watch as Noah's face tumbles like I've just thrown his joy off a cliff.

"Come with me to the lake," he says suddenly, and I start to protest. Noah holds up his hands. "I already ordered you a milkshake and a burger. Let's grab it and go to the lake, just to eat. Give me an hour, Never Regali, and I will make it worth your while."

"God, Noah, I can't," I say, but I want to cry when I say it. Noah turns around and I swear to God, some of that pretty, practiced perfection slips. I watch his shoulders rise and fall as he breathes. He's wearing a white and blue striped button up with short sleeves over a white tee. He's paired it with a pair of blue jeans and some Converse. Light, unobtrusive. Noah was never one to take his looks very seriously. Anyway, maybe that was a luxury of being born pretty because Noah Scott is drop dead gorgeous. Still, he never minced his words and he was always poetic, even at his dirtiest. He turns back towards me, and I can see that my leaving has left this mark on his soul that cannot be erased. For good or bad, he and I are part of one another and might be forever. I have to talk this out with him, for both our sakes. And for Ty's. If I choose Ty because I refuse to see Noah, what good does that do? I have to choose Ty for Ty and in spite of Noah. I have to.

"Please," Noah begs, but I'm already decided. "I can't move on, Never. I've been so stuck without you." I close my eyes against tears.

"Okay," I say. "Okay, but just for a little while, Noah, and I'm not promising anything."

"Thank you," he breathes, and I feel guilty because he sounds so relieved. "Thank you, Never. You have no idea how much this means to me." But I do. I do because it might even mean more to me than it does to him.

13

I let Noah drive because I don't know if I can right now. Besides, I trust him. Even though it's been five years since we've seen each other, I know that Noah would never do anything to hurt me or make me uncomfortable. If I ask him, he'll take me back to the Dairy Queen.

"You haven't touched your shake?" he says with a smile, finally breaking a ten minute stretch of moonlit silence. When I don't answer, Noah focuses his attention back on the road and turns on his blinker. The lake isn't far from the Dairy

Queen which isn't far from downtown which isn't far from my mother's house. This town is small, too small in my opinion, but it does have its perks. One of which is that Noah and I don't have to suffer in awkward silence for too, too long before we get to the empty parking lot by the lake. Even in the dead of night, even though nobody friggin' cares, Noah Scott puts money into the machine that dispenses parking passes and puts one under his windshield wiper. I look at the car, examine the sleek black curves, and wonder how much it set his Daddy back. Mr. Scott is very well to do, so I'm guessing the number is something astronomical, more than my tuition probably. I hate the world for that. I hate that Ty had to sell his body to make ends meet while Mr. Scott plays games with his money like the earth is one big, giant Monopoly board, sits back and reaps the benefits. I fucking hate that. But I don't hate Noah. Noah was never the spoiled, little rich kid archetype. He's always been thoughtful and poetic. I see that time hasn't changed that.

"*In darkness they were born and in darkness they bled, one for the other, two souls lost in a sea of black until finally, they found a beam of light and that they followed until they hit the sun and were reborn.*" Noah pauses and looks over his shoulder at me. "Sorry," he says, but I've finally got a smile on my face. "Might be a little much if I start quoting poetry at you from minute one."

"That's okay," I say as we both step over the small, wooden fence that separates the parking lot from the grassy area surrounding Shadow Lake. It's still just as beautiful as I remember, but not as beautiful as the sea. I hate that I can see the other side, although distant. The ocean offers up so many more possibilities. It might be more dangerous, but I like it better than the lake, even if it's the safer choice. "I missed your poems." I pause as I think about how to tell Noah that I kind of stalked him. "Well, I missed hearing you recite them. I read all the ones you posted," I say as we move over to a picnic table and sit on the top with our feet on the bench, backs towards the parking lot and eyes focused on the still, quiet waters of the lake.

"I looked everywhere for you, Never," he whispers and his voice carries across the surface of the lake like a dragonfly. "You didn't post anything online, nothing to let me know you were there, that you were listening." Noah pauses. "Did you read my Butterfly Series?" he asks referring to a set of poems that I printed out and read until the paper fell apart, until my eyes were blurry. I know all about the Butterfly Series.

"Alas! I've discovered the crisis of humanity; a dirty truth is no better than a pretty lie yet one is substantially more harsh than the other. How can I, a man without a heart, be expected to tell either without crippling his soul beyond repair?" I quote Noah's words without a hitch, without a single stumble, and finally give in to the smell of the food, stuffing a cold fry into my mouth and sucking at the straw to my milkshake. Noah looks at me for a long moment, and then he reaches out and brushes some hair from my face. I feel paralyzed, so I don't move. I just sit there and watch him watching me and don't know what to do.

"To answer your question," he says finally as he turns his head away from me and leans back on his palms. "When I woke up and found you had left, I … " Noah freezes, and I take the chance to examine the smooth, straight line of his nose, his perfect, pink lips and the way he runs his tongue across them unconsciously. He's not as muscular as Ty, but he's strong. I can see it in his arms, the way his shirt falls neatly down the smooth plane of his belly. I remember touching it, running my fingers down it, licking my way to his cock. My first and last blow job. I didn't do blow jobs with my guy friends. What was the point? Get them off while I sit there and watch, wallowing in my pain? No, thank you. I needed to fill that hole inside of me. I look away, suddenly ashamed. *Noah doesn't know. Noah doesn't know. He doesn't know. He doesn't know I'm a fucking whore, but what if he did? How do I tell him? Do I have to tell him?* I swing my gaze back to Noah and my chip earring hits me again. I want to rip it out and throw it in the lake, but I know that's stupid, that I'd regret that, so I just touch it, still its movement before Noah sees and asks about it. "I panicked Never," Noah finally admits. "I panicked because I loved you so much I thought my heart was going to explode every time you walked into a room. I wanted to marry you, have a family with you, keep you forever."

"I'm not a dog," I snap, and feel instantly guilty. Obviously Noah is aware of that fact. His face falls, and I find myself reaching out to apologize. I touch the back of his hand gently and have to swallow three times before I can speak. "I'm sor-"

"I still love you, Never."

Shit.

"Noah," I begin because I can't stand having these two guys saying things like this to me. It makes me feel ... strange. I went from empty inside to full all at once, and I don't know how to handle it. Noah holds up his hands.

"I'm sorry. I shouldn't have said that," he tells me softly and tries to smile his way through the awkward. It works. I smile back. "Let's start over." Noah takes a deep breath and sets his hands on his knees. "So," he begins. "How the hell have you been?" I look at Noah, practically sparkling in the fucking moonlight, and I know I can't tell him anything real, not now, not yet. Fuck, maybe not ever. I can't tell him that I've had sex with more men than I can count on both hands and both feet, that my family chose a murderer over me, that the *only* friends I've made in five friggin' years are Lacey Setter and Ty McCabe. Ty McCabe. I definitely can't tell him about Ty McCabe.

"I'm going to school," I say vaguely because I'm used to being vague with people. It takes a lot for me to really open up, to give out pieces of myself. I used to have no problem with that, especially when Noah was on the receiving end, but now … Things are so different. "In California." Noah is waiting patiently, certain that I'm getting to something more relevant, more personal. He's too trusting. I wonder if I was ever that trusting and shiver. Noah thinks it's from the cold and slips his arm around my waist, just like he used to do when we were in high school. In fact, I get hit so hard with déjà vu that I can barely breathe. I don't resist him even though I know I should, even though I know that I might be giving him the wrong idea.

"Me, too," he says simply. "Here in town, though. I … " Noah looks away from me and out at the lake. "I didn't want to leave in case you came back. Somehow, someday, I knew you would." Noah pauses. "I guess I was right." I don't respond to that. There's this unspoken phrase hanging in the air. *I knew you'd come back for me.* I don't correct him, tell him that I'm actually here for myself, to put me back together and make things right. I go for a cigarette and am not surprised to see Noah's nose wrinkle. He never liked it when I smoked. Back then though, I only ever smoked a couple a day. Now, now I think I'd have to consider myself a chain smoker. I just can't stop. Every stressful impulse I have makes me crazy. It's either smoke or fuck. That's all there is to it. Noah watches me light up, but he doesn't pull his arm away. He sits there and lets smoke taint his expensive shirt, his pretty blonde hair, his angelic face.

Finding Never - 75

"I got a dog," he says randomly, and I smile. "An Australian Shepherd that bites." I laugh and have to snatch at my cig to keep it from hitting the table. I slip it back between my lips and talk around it, the way Ty always does.

"What's she look like?" I ask wishing I could get a dog. I think a dog would be good for me. A constant companion, one who doesn't judge, someone that loves me for me always and forever. Yeah, I think I'll get a dog. I'll have to move out of the dorms but whatever. I kind of hate it there anyway. I want my own bathroom. I get this strange image of Ty and me sharing a place, maybe even having Lacey as a roommate. There's a fireplace and a bed for two, a bed that's always full and never empty. Always full of Ty. Ty. Ty. Ty. I shake my head to clear it.

"She's mostly white with orange splotches over her eyes and gray down her back. I think you'd like her quite a bit. She's almost as ornery as you." I chuckle again and don't tell Noah that I like mutts a thousand times better than purebreds. I want a grungy, nasty alley dog like the Tramp from that Disney movie. I want a dog that's been behind bars with a missing leg and a grin that doesn't stop. I want a dog whose parents were so mixed, they were like rainbows, a bit of every color. Noah's dog, however nice, is no doubt from some, spoiled privileged breeder who feeds her pets raw rabbit and lets them sleep on goose down beds covered in silk. "Want to meet her?" he asks, and I shrug noncommittally. I don't know where this is going, so I have to keep my options open. "Maybe tomorrow I could take you out, bring her along, and we could go for a hike along the river, like the good ol' days?" His offer is too good to refuse. I want to walk along the banks without shoes and listen to the roar of water. Yes, yes, I'll go.

"Sure," I say before I can question myself. There are a lot of factors to consider here, least of which has a nose ring and a wicked smile. My sisters won't want me to go; I won't want to leave them. But I'm going to do it anyway because my questions about Noah Scott have not been answered. He's still a big, fat question mark. "What's her name?" I ask him. "Your dog?" Noah laughs and shakes his head like he can't believe he's about to say this.

"It's Never," he says. "Her name is Never."

14

When I get back to my mother's house, Ty is sitting on the front steps with a cigarette between his sexy lips. His eyes are closed, and he's leaning back with his elbows on the faded wood of the porch. He doesn't move when he hears me pull the truck back up to the barn, doesn't look at me when I climb out and crunch across the ground towards him. I pause with my tennis shoes inches from Ty's boots and wait.

I smile then I worry that Ty will think the expression is for Noah and frown.

"Have a good time?" he asks softly, voice low and dangerous, like he could explode into motion at the drop of a hat. His muscles are so tense that they're making mine cramp in sympathy. Ty cracks his eyes and glances up at me as a bit of ash falls on his chest. He's not even smoking the damn cig. I meet his gaze and sigh.

"Kind of," I say, feeling bad for being so late. I didn't mean to stay out so long. It's just ... being with Noah was kind of magical, like I was a different person in a different world with a different life. I didn't expect that. And after the reception I'd gotten from my mother, I didn't expect him to be so damn happy to see me. "We went out to this lake that we used to go to as kids and just talked, caught up, you know?"

"Yeah?" Ty asks, and I can tell that he's fucking terrified that I'm going to run away with Noah Scott, make little blonde babies, and move into that horribly ostentatious McMansion that Noah's parents built. I kick the bottom of his shoe.

"Sorry," I tell him as I wrinkle my nose. I'm not a complete idiot. I realize that leaving my new pseudo-boyfriend/sex addict sponsor/best friend/pain in the ass at the home of my family who I haven't seen in years was a bit of a strange thing to do. I *had* to see Noah though, and I think Ty understands that. What he won't understand and what I don't know how to explain is that I have a ... thing ... with Noah tomorrow. A date? No, it isn't a date, but what is it? I also didn't tell Noah about Ty, so I imagine that tomorrow, when he comes to pick me up, that there will be trouble. Especially when I tell him that Ty is coming with us.

Fuck me.

"Lacey texted me," Ty says mildly. I can tell he wants to ask more questions about Noah but doesn't know how. "She wants you to know that she and Trini are like, totally official now." I snort at Ty's imitation of Lacey's voice. He finally inhales and pulls the cigarette out of his mouth so he can speak properly. "Never ... "

"I didn't sleep with him," I promise and Ty pauses, bracelets jingling as he drops the cigarette to the dirt. "All we did was hug." Ty nods and pushes himself to his feet with a grunt. I watch him stretch his arms above his head, bangle bracelets sliding down his arms towards his elbow as he lifts his hands and tangles his fingers together.

"I'm glad, Never," he says as he drops his arms and steps forward, takes my chin in his fingers and kisses me, lips like a butterfly's wings, ever so soft against my own. I sigh into him and lean forward so that my head is cradled in the nook of Ty's neck. He squeezes me tight and runs his ringed fingers through my hair. Miraculously, they never get caught. "I am so fucking glad."

"Ty," I say as he holds me ever so tightly. "Thanks for putting up with me." At this I get a laugh, a real genuine, knock your socks off kind of a laugh. Ty pulls back and pokes me in the forehead with a ringed finger.

"Don't be stupid," he says as he cocks his head to the side. "You're not a girl that any guy could just put up with. You're a fucking whirlwind, Never." I don't know if this is a compliment or not, but I do remember that Ty told me he loved me. I'm guessing those feelings haven't disappeared in the last few days, so I smile and pull out a cigarette and a lighter. If my mom's still the same hypocritical bitch that she's always been, then if I smoke in the house, she'll have a fit. Weird for a chain smoker. I'd always thought that. Now that I'm one, too, I can't understand it. It's like she's ashamed to admit her faults, like she doesn't want anyone to know that she smokes. I want everyone to know. If they want to hate me for it, good for them.

India opens the screen door and smiles warmly at us. I can

tell that she's been waiting anxiously for me, and I feel guilty about how much time I spent with Noah.

"Everyone's asleep, but I thought I should tell you that Mom unlocked your room."

"Unlocked my room?" I ask, completely and utterly baffled. India nods and scoops some copper hair behind her ear. She's got this gorgeous purple eyeshadow around her eyes that make them sparkle like diamonds. Tomorrow, before I go out with Noah, I'm going to ask her how she puts it on.

"Yeah, um … " she nibbles her lip while Ty steals my cigarette and finishes it. India shrugs like she isn't sure how to say what she wants to say and motions us inside. "Just … come in." I look at Ty who shrugs and follow her into the warm house. India locks the door behind us and flicks off the living room lights before leading us up the stairs to the second floor. From what I've seen thus far, the house is virtually the same. There are family portraits on the wall above the stairs that Ty stares at as we walk past. I glance at them, but they're the same ones I saw a thousand times as a kid. If asked, I could replicate them all in perfect detail with just a pen and paper. The memories are that clear.

India turns right and stops at the first door. It's white with a big, black scrawl that supposedly says *Never.* I wrote it with Sharpie in a teenage rage, so it's barely legible. Beneath it, crayon drawings galore wash the wood with color.

"Maple," India explains and I feel myself brighten at the thought of my niece and my new baby sister, Darla. They're young enough that I could still have a relationship with them if I tried. Things aren't all bad. Angelica Regali may be a lost cause, and after the way she treated me I kind of hope she gets torn apart by wild dogs, but there is still life here to be salvaged. I can smell it. India pushes the door open, flicks the light on, and steps back.

What I see takes my breath away. My room is *unchanged*. And not just in the way that the furniture is the same or the posters or the carpet ... I mean *everything* has been left exactly the same as the day I left. I even see my hot pink sweatshirt with the hole in the armpit, the one that Noah Scott gently slipped over my head before he kissed the living daylights out of me and made love to me in the very same bed that I'm now staring at. I left him lying there naked and although the bed is now made, the blankets, the pillows, the sheets are all the same. I stumble back and Ty catches me under the arms before I fall to my knees. My head is spinning like crazy and I feel sick.

"I don't ... understand," I say as I try to wrap my mind around this. "But ... there are only seven bedrooms ... " I trail off and wait for India to explain. She looks nervous, like this whole thing is weird for her, too.

"The day you left, Noah came downstairs and told Mom that you'd run away. At first, she was pissed off, but later ... " India trails off, and I suddenly feel so bad for her that I can't breathe. I hurt her so bad without even realizing I was doing it. She had nothing to do with the problems that chased me away, and I don't know how I'm ever going to be able to ask for her forgiveness. "Later, she got weird. One day she just came up here, made your bed, and closed the door. She locked it and that was that. Never," India says tentatively as she glances at Ty and tries to judge exactly what he is to me. Whatever she sees there gives her confidence, and I vow to remember the look on my sister's face. *Relaxed.* She likes Ty. Good. "Nobody's been in here since except maybe Mom. She never unlocked it, not once."

"So ... " I struggle to understand why my room has been left to collect dust while my sisters continue to share. India rushes to explain, gesturing with her thin fingers and pale hands like she can't talk fast enough to get the information out, like maybe she could sign it if she wanted.

"Beth and Maple share a room, and Lettie took Zella's room when she moved out. Lorri and Darla share. It's not so bad, Never. We were glad to leave it. As long as it was here, it was like you could come back somehow, like if we waited long enough, you'd appear here in your baggy sweatshirts and your butterfly clips." India starts to cry as Ty sets me up straight and gives me a gentle nudge in the direction of my little sister. I take her in my arms and try not to let too many tears fall into her pretty hair.

"I'm sorry, India," I tell her. "I'm so sorry." She shakes her head and pulls back, wiping her arm across her face with a sniffle. She might be sixteen, but she's a young sixteen. I vow then and there to protect India from the hell I went through. I don't want her to understand what I did or why. I want her to grow up happy and blissfully fucking ignorant. I want her to dream of cherry blossoms and puppies and love at first sight.

"I know," she whispers. "I know why you left." I open my mouth to explain, but India raises both hands and backs away. When she looks up, she's smiling.

"You don't have to explain, Never. I know all about Luis." I cringe when I hear that man's name. He doesn't deserve a name, doesn't even deserve a life, but he has one and my daddy doesn't. That's a problem, a real big one. Before I leave this town of secrets and betrayal, I have to find Luis, preferably with Ty by my side. Maybe he can punch him out the way he did the robber in the convenience store. That, at least, would be satisfying to watch.

"Do you know where he is?" I ask India, convinced that she's the only one who would be willing to tell me. She bites her lip again and nods.

"In town. I don't know where specifically, but I usually see his truck outside Broken Glass." I glance over at Ty.

"The watering hole for stupid ass, drunk fucks," I explain and India laughs.

"Why? You're not thinking of – " The door at the end of the hallway swings open and Beth pokes her head out. Her hair is wrapped up in a blue handkerchief with flowers on it, making her look a million years older than she really is.

"Never," she says. "I love you like a doll and tomorrow, I'm going to pick your brain, but unless you want to get to know your new niece by staying up with her all night, I suggest you guys keep it down and go to bed." Beth starts to retreat back into her room and pauses. "You'll still be here?" She takes a big breath. "In the morning, I mean. You're not leaving anytime soon, are you?"

"I'm here as long as I want to be here," I say and then add, "As long as it doesn't interfere with school." Beth smiles at me. She might be annoying and tactless, and she might not have believed me about Luis, but she's glad I'm here. I can see that.

"Good girl," she says. "I always knew you were smart." And then she closes her door softly. India smiles at me, at Ty.

"I guess I'll see you tomorrow?" she asks tentatively. I nod and touch the side of her face, glad to be back, glad that I can share this simple, quiet moment with my sister. "Good. Because I want to hear how the two of you met." India spins on her heel and moves down the hallway with practiced steps, quiet as a mouse. *How we met,* I think, remembering the little incident at the bar and the big incident at the convenience store. Somehow, someway, that quick fuck I was looking for turned into this incredible soul with a sultry smile and rough, calloused hands that feel as soft as feathers in the bedroom.

"Come on," I say to Ty as I grab his hand and pull him back in time. "Come meet Never Regali."

15

My room might have remained unaltered, but it was not left untouched. There's not a speck of dust to be found anywhere. It puts some coins in my mother's bank and buys her another chance, one more chance to care about me because she must if she took the time to maintain this warp in time.

I run my hands over my dresser and find a brooch that Noah gave me for our one year anniversary. I pick it up and drop it in a jewelry box I barely remember owning. I don't want to answer any questions about it. Ty already has a thousand crouching behind his eyes. I can see them dancing as his eyes sweep over the posters on my wall and ceiling, past the broken mirror next to the bathroom door, across the pages of scribbled notes I tacked above my desk.

"This is so fucking weird," I laugh as I shake my head and try to make sense of my feelings. So much is happening so fast, I don't even know where to begin with myself, let alone Ty. "I mean, does this make any sense to you?" Ty touches my pink sweatshirt, rubs the fabric between his fingers.

"I kind of wanted to punch your mom in the face for you earlier, but seeing this," Ty looks up and then swings his gaze around to find mine. "Makes me think she deserves another chance." I smile.

"Great minds think alike," I tell him as he moves across the room towards me. The air heats with this pulsing energy that intensifies exponentially with each movement Ty makes. He doesn't touch me, but he does get close enough that I can feel the warmth of his body.

"This is the first time we've been alone since you ran out on me."

"Shut up," I say, but I can't argue with that because it's true.

"I love you Never Ross," he says and my heart swells strangely, gets so big that it crushes my lungs and strangles me. "And I think I love Never Regali, too. Or I would if," Ty shows me something in his hand. My vision flickers. *Fuck.*

It's the naughty, little nightgown I bought for Noah, the one that I lost my virginity in. Ty's found it and now he has it in his hand. He's grinning and his dimples are deep as pits. I can't refuse, can't let him know where it came from or why I had it. Silently, I lift my arms above my head and hope I don't pass out.

Ty finds my skin under my shirt and slides his fingers up, taking both the shirt and sweater along with them. He tosses them over my computer chair and drops the nightgown over my head. The silky fabric slithers down my skin and hits me just above the knees. It's a beautiful piece of lingerie, blood red and charged for sex. I close my eyes for a moment and try to keep myself from venturing too far down memory lane.

"Undress me," Ty whispers. "I promised you that you'd get a turn." My mouth goes dry; my hands sweat, and I feel like that long ago girl who had no idea how powerful sex was, how easily it can be abused. It's like a drug, something that I never should've started without understanding the consequences. I step back and Ty's face locks up in fear. He's so fucking scared of me. Maybe I'm not the only one at risk of breaking here? Maybe Ty is just as vulnerable to me as I am to him?

I smile as I reach under the nightgown and unbutton my jeans, dropping them to the floor as I kick off my shoes and finally peel off my socks. Ty is smiling now, too, and I know that I'm going to have to be careful with him. He might be a bad boy, but even bad boys can be broken.

"You know what?" I tell him as I move forward and curl my fingers in his shirt. "There's something I always fantasized about as a teenager. Want to make a dirty girl's dreams come true?" I pull Ty's shirt up and over his head, barely making it past his arms before he's pulling me to him, grabbing me by the back of the neck and kissing my mouth hot and hungry. I can already feel his erection through his jeans, hard and desperate for me. I hope we can make it outside.

"This better be good," Ty growls. "Because I've been looking at you for days but not touching. That wasn't easy." He pauses, and I think we both remember the scene on the bus. "Well, okay, maybe that isn't completely true, but it sure as fuck feels like it." I don't remind him of the weeks we spent together without touching or the fact that we're both still sex addicts, I just grab him by the hand and drag him down the stairs. From memory, I know that the third step from the bottom is a creaky one and warn Ty. He raises his eyebrows at this. "So you've always been a bad girl?" he asks, but he smiles when he says it and we make it outside without getting caught by any of my estranged family members.

I pause when my feet hit the dirt and spin around to face Ty, running my hands down his perfect chest. I haven't had a chance to explore it to my liking, so I'm going to trace every muscle a hundred times over until I've memorized the rise and fall of his abs. It will give me something special to hold in my heart, something that separates him even further from the rest of the boys I've slept with. I will learn *all* of Ty's nooks and crannies, imperfections, desires.

"Take off your shoes," I tell him, and he raises his dark brows at me. He doesn't know the power the earth holds here, the way it can ground you like nothing else. The Northwest is beautiful, but it doesn't hold the same quality, the same goodness-gracious-I-am-so-fucking-home feeling. Ty doesn't argue because he gets it, like always. He sits down on the porch steps and pulls off his boots. He isn't wearing any socks underneath. I smile. "I hope that means you're not wearing any underwear either?" I ask as he stands up and puts a cigarette between his lips. Ty grins, nice and wicked, his expression sharp enough to cut.

"Well," he says as he steps forward and wraps his arms around me, sliding them down the satin nightgown until he's cupping my bare ass. "Guess I could ask you the same question." I try to speak, to say something cheeky like, *But you already know the answer,* except I can't. My skin is tingling at Ty's touch; his hands are making my blood sing, and I just can't force the words past my lips. "You know," he tells me as he breathes against my ear and makes me shiver. "I could throw you down right here and fuck you. What do you say?" I swallow and don't say any of the things I'm thinking. *Brilliant. Yes. God, please do.*

"Come with me," I choke out as I search Ty's face, try to peel back some layers and see what's lying underneath. Never before have I descended into the mind of someone who's as dark, if not darker, than I am, and it's fascinating. Or at least I think it is. Ty knows what I'm doing, and he doesn't let me dig very deep, not yet.

"Okay," he says finally. I grab his hand and pull him around the barn that we've never used, take him past the rusted cars that used to belong to my father and around the back where long, golden grasses stretch as far as the eye can see, punctuated by the dark shadow of a single house. Otherwise, it's just us. Just me and Ty alone with the whispering wind and our pasts that are now so tangled together that I don't know if they can be separated without killing one or both of us.

"Tell me," I say to him as he flicks the lighter and his eyes dance with flames. "Are we going back to SOG?" Ty shrugs and lets his head fall back. His eyes flicker closed and he inhales deeply. His throat is smooth and perfect with just the slightest hint of an Adam's apple, muscular with the briefest glimmer of butterfly wings. They trail down his shoulders and arm, fade into the birds that line his back.

"Depends," he tells me as he drops his chin and hands the cigarette to me.

"On?" I ask as I take it and slide it between my moist lips. Ty steps towards me and puts his hands on either side of my face.

"On you," he whispers against my lips. "All I need is you. You're my cure."

"Ty," I say as I try to step back, but he doesn't let me. He runs his hands down my arms, touching me so slightly that I swear I can feel the whorls of his fingertips against the fine hairs on my skin. "Don't say things like that," I tell him. I don't want to be his cure. He can't let so much ride on me. I'm unstable. I'm just … so fucked up. I can't be Ty McCabe's chance at salvation. He's been making it for himself, for me. He has to keep doing that or neither of us will survive this.

"Never," he tells me, voice strong but quiet. "I love you." My heart chokes on his words, and I try to pull back, but Ty won't let me. I don't know it yet, but Ty will never let me go. For better or worse, I think he's my soul mate. I might not understand what that means yet, but I will. Oh God, I will, because Ty won't let me run away from it.

"Stop it," I whisper as the cigarette slips out from between my teeth and hits the dirt. "You can't keep saying things like that."

"Why not?" he asks me, unashamed, unabashed at his words. "You said it, too." Ty grins at me. "Say it again," he commands, but I can't form the words. They slipped out before at the bus station. I can't say them again, not yet.

"I can't," I whisper, and I wonder if he's going to get upset or hurt or angry. I'm afraid to find out, so I blurt, "Come see my fantasy?" Ty smiles and follows me over to an old tractor. It sits in a clear bit of dirt, rusty and perfect in the moonlight like a solid, corporeal memory of my father. I have hardly any in my head, so it's nice to see one sitting here undisturbed. I'm surprised my mother never sold it. "This," I say as I put my hand on one of the big rear tires. "Is a 1951 Farmall 'Super C' vintage tractor." Ty whistles and steps up beside me.

"I love a girl that can talk shop," he says as he runs his ringed hand over the metal with a gentle touch that tells me he senses how important this thing is. "Now, tell me, how does this hunk of junk play into your fantasies?" Ty asks with a wink. I spin slowly, follow him as he walks around me and continues around the front of the tractor like a predator circling prey. It's kind of hot.

"Listen to me, Ty McCabe," I say, feeling bold in the white moonlight. Her touch gives me strength and banishes the demons, at least temporarily. "When I was in high school, I used to entertain thoughts about this tractor." I pause. "And about a guy fucking me on it." Ty's brows shoot up and he pauses across from me, facing my body with his own. I can practically feel the electricity in the air between us, sizzling, getting ready to shock us both if we're not careful.

"I see," he says, voice low and husky.

"So, what are you waiting for?" I ask him. "Fuck me on it."

Ty doesn't waste another moment. He steps forward and spins me around like a dancer, putting his hand on the center of my back and pushing me over so that I have to grab two bars on the back of the tractor to stay upright. My heart begins to pulse, heats my blood, makes my entire body go limp under Ty's touch.

"You are one, dirty girl," he growls as he pushes my nightgown up my sides and lets it hang in blood red folds around my waist. My chip earring slaps my cheek, but I ignore it. I'm not having sex to fill a void or because I'm lonely or to wake myself up inside. I'm having sex because I want to have sex. With Ty. Only with Ty. I hear him unzip his pants as I stare down at the dirty ground and hope none of my sisters look out the windows and see us. If they do, it'll make an awkward morning even worse.

I'm having sex to have sex. Might not seem like a strange concept to you, but it is downright frightening to me. I close my eyes and try not to groan as Ty slides the hardness of his cock against me, just enough to tease but not enough to release any of the pressure inside of me.

"Say it," he tells me, and it takes me a second to realize what he wants.

"Later," I say, and I'm embarrassed to hear my voice come out in a whimper. Ty squeezes my hips hard and I can feel the impression of his rings against my skin. Neither of us remembers to use a condom. We never have, and old habits die hard. Plus, we're both clean, so I suppose it doesn't really matter. Besides, the idea that other woman have gotten to feel Ty's hard cock warm and bare inside them pisses me off. Why should I have to have a piece of rubber separating us? I think all of these weird things in the back of my mind. In the front of it, I'm wondering what's taking a stud like Ty so fucking long to get to it.

"Not until you say it," he whispers cruelly as he grinds his hips into my ass. I try to stand up, but I can't escape. Ty McCabe has me trapped, physically, mentally, emotionally. Tears sting my eyes. He has no idea how hard this is for me or maybe he does, I don't know. If I say it again, if I admit that I love him, then I'm only going to be emphasizing how much hold he has over me.

"I can't," I whisper as wet drops hit the earth and pool into little balls, drawn together by cohesion, much like Ty and my tortured bits are drawn together, desperate to cling to one another, like to like, pain to pain.

"Yes, you can," he whispers as he slides into me, buries his warmth deep within my soul, makes me cry out as my hands squeeze tight around the rusty metal. "Say it." Ty pushes himself all the way in so that our bodies are locked together in a swirl of painful pleasure that makes me bite my lip hard. One, single drop of blood hits the earth as I gasp and try to draw a full breath. I feel so full that I don't know if there's room inside of me for air. There's just enough room for Ty and his twisted, dark, fucked up beauty. Ty waits for a moment and then begins to move, sliding himself in and out of me with slow, careful strokes that feel more like torture than anything else.

"Ty McCabe," I gasp as he starts to breathe heavy behind me. "You are cruel in more ways than one."

"And Never Ross," he says through a groan. "You owe me big time."

I stare at the earth through tears and wonder if I'm going to cry every time Ty fucks me. I hope not, but then you never know with me. You Never fucking know. Ty's moans pick up in pitch, matching mine, syllable for syllable, until we're in perfect unison, like some sort of carnal chorus, crying out our pleasure and pain for the moon and the stars to hear. Before I know it, I'm saying the words he wants me to say, and I'm meaning them, fully and completely and without regret.

"I love you," I say as the heat takes over me and spills down my skin, singes my heart and burns my soul. "I love you, Ty McCabe."

16

Ty and I are too fucking tired to carry on anymore heart to hearts that night, so we fall asleep together in my old bed, arms wrapped tightly around one another. Ty falls into a dead sleep almost immediately, but not me. I drift in and out for awhile until I decide that it's just too much trouble and give up. I'm too fucking freaked out at what's happening between us to let my mind relax completely. I have Ty's naked body next to mine, every warm inch of it pressing against my skin. I can hear his breathing and feel his chest rising and falling. It's such a new, frightening experience that I have a difficult time adjusting. We did this once before, after we made love, but my emotions were so up in the air that I can hardly remember. It's so hazy and foggy and distant seeming.

I keep my head on Ty's chest, let him tangle his hand in my hair and stare out the window at the night sky for God only knows how long. My brain cannot stop imagining possibilities and what-ifs and maybes. I slip out of bed after awhile, exhausted but conflicted and dig through my bag looking for something comfortable to wear. I settle on a pair of sweats and a baggy tee and make my way down the stairs to find the front door wide open.

My mother is sitting on the porch steps with a cigarette in her mouth. I stare at the back of her head for a long, long while debating the risks of going out there. I close my eyes and touch my chest. I can still feel Ty's energy swirling around inside of me, and it gives me just enough strength to make my decision.

"Still smoking American Spirits, I see," I say as I move outside on quiet feet and sit down next to Angelica the Selfish. She chuckles, and I can't help but notice how pretty my mama is. Sitting in the starlight with her copper curls down her back, she looks ten years younger than she did earlier. I try not to think mean things like *Maybe she sucks the youth out of all the young men she sleeps with,* but the thoughts come unbidden and sit there as I reluctantly accept a cig from her outstretched hand.

"Why did you come back?" she asks me all casual like. She's still the only person that hasn't hugged me or cried. I force myself to think about the lack of dust in my bedroom and know that she has feelings for me whether she shows them or not. I use my mother's blue lighter and watch as the lit cherry makes her cheeks glow like they've been rouged. I turn away from her and rest my elbows on my knees as I think about an answer to that question.

"To piece myself back together," I respond honestly. "To get the closure I never had. To find out why a murderer meant more to you than I did." I give her no holds barred honesty and watch her face. She says nothing.

"Do you like Darla?" she asks instead as she looks over at me and examines my face like she's never seen it before. "She looks just like you when you were a baby."

"Where is he, Mom?" I ask, inquiring about Luis. "Why isn't he here anymore? What happened?" My mom shakes her head and tries to stand up, but I grab her hand and plead with everything inside of me that she'll be a Mom for one second, just one. "Please, tell me," I whisper as she stares down at me. The crickets mark the passing of time with gentle chirps, letting us know that no matter what is happening to us, the world is still spinning whether we like it or not.

"He tried to touch your sister," she says, and my blood goes cold.

"What?" One single word burning with the world's hottest malice.

"Oh for God's sake, Never. That was four years ago, and I don't want to talk about it." Mom pulls her hand away from me, but I don't let her leave. I get up and follow after her, taking my cigarette along with me.

"But I do," I say. "I want to talk about it." Angelica Regali shakes her head and moves into the kitchen. I chase after her and refuse to let this go. I can't. I just can't. "Who? When? What happened?"

"He's already been dealt with, Never," my mother says as she pours herself some Scotch. "It's over and done with.

Don't think you can come riding in on a white horse and save everyone from themselves. It's not going to happen. Just because you spent time on the West Coast doesn't mean you know everything all of a sudden."

"Oh fuck, Mom," I say, throwing my hands in the air. "Are you really gonna go there? Are you really going to play the region game with me? This is such bullshit. I'm not trying to save anyone from anything. I just want to know what the motherfucker did to my sister."

"If you cared," she says, spinning around with her glass of alcohol raised between us like a shield. "You'd have stuck around." I see red, bloody, violent, angry red. I want to scream, but I want to keep this conversation away from my sisters, so I don't. I take a deep breath and imagine Ty. Somehow, that works, and I start to calm down.

"Who?" I ask, certain that at least she'll give me that bit of information. My mother sighs and glares at the tip of my cigarette like it's the devil come to take her home to where she belongs.

"Jade."

"Did he rape her?" My mind is so cold right now, so empty behind all of this red rage in my vision. It's a strange place to be, and I don't like it. It makes me afraid of myself, afraid of what I might do. My mom doesn't answer, just stands there and drinks her booze. I stare, and I wait, and I wait. Jade was Luis' biological daughter which makes this all the more disturbing to me. I start to pace.

"No, Never. He didn't get that far." I spin around. One question hangs from my lips.

"Why?"

"Because he got caught. We already pressed charges, Never. He spent a few months in jail. What else do you want me to do? Go punish him myself?"

"I want you to tell me exactly what happened, and I want you to tell me you're sorry, that I was right, that I've always been right and that you were dead wrong." Tears start to spill down my cheeks again. "I want you to tell me that you love me, Mom. Here's your chance. I am giving you a one time, get out of jail free card. Help me move on. Be my mother for once."

Angelica looks me right in the face before she breaks my heart.

"I'm sorry, Never, but I can't. I can't right now."

And then she moves away and I fall to my knees on the linoleum floor, shattered to pieces and desperate for help.

Thirty seconds later, Ty walks in and saves me from myself.

17

"Oh, Never," Ty says, sitting down beside me. "Fuck."

I've stopped crying which is a bad sign. I go to that empty place inside of myself, the one that always used to cry out for pretend love, and try to get a hold of myself. Ty doesn't wait for me to say anything or explain, he just reaches out and pulls me into his lap, squeezes me tight against his bare chest and holds me there. I cling to him and breathe through my nose. I want to get better, I want to change, I want a life where I don't cry at night, where I stop pushing people away, that I can live without regrets.

"She doesn't love me." The statement is simple enough to understand, but Ty shakes his head.

"She does," he explains as I try to push back from him. He won't let me. Somehow, in this moment he knows better what I need than I do.

"Did you fucking hear that conversation?" I ask, and Ty nods.

"I see a woman who's afraid, afraid to love, afraid to admit to her mistakes because then she has to take the blame for the pain in her daughters' lives, and she isn't strong enough for that."

"How do you know that?" I ask him. "You just fucking met her." Ty lets me move back and stares at me with dark eyes. Something is coming, something big. "Don't," I say before any words can come from Ty's lips. "Stop."

"When I was twelve, my step-father tried to rape me."

"Ty ... " He isn't ready for this, and I don't want him spilling his secrets because he feels sorry for me. That isn't right. If I let him do that, I'll be as bad as Angelica.

"Luckily, he didn't quite make it all the way, but ... " Ty nibbles his lip ring and sighs. "The point is, my mom didn't believe me." He pauses. "Sorry, scratch that. Let me rephrase it. She knew I was telling the truth, but she didn't want to admit that to herself." I put my hands over my ears and close my eyes. Ty cannot open himself up for me or his heart may fall out. I can't have that happening. I don't want him to slide back because I'm having such a hard time moving forward.

"Stop," I whisper in the quiet dark of the kitchen. "Don't break yourself into pieces for me."

"Never," Ty says as he gently but firmly moves my hands

away from my ears. "I will do whatever it takes to make you better, even if it means destroying myself in the process."

"But why?" I whisper. *You're not worth it,* rings through my head, but I push it back. That's not Ty, not anymore. He was just reacting to me back then; now he's reacting for me.

"I told you, Never, I fucking love you."

"You don't even know me."

"Bullshit." Ty drops my hands and looks at me with an expression that says he's not taking any shit. "Don't be stupid, Nev. You know better than anyone that that's not true. You're the only person in the world that's ever known me. Maybe we haven't known each other since high school," I notice the slightest bite in Ty's words, the slightest punch of anger for Noah Scott. "But that doesn't fucking matter. Relationships can't be measured with a clock or a calendar, Never. It's about getting each other. You get me, and I get you. That's the only thing I give a shit about."

"I don't deserve you," I say and mean it. Ty smiles and pulls me into his lap, lifts me up and carries me like some fucking fairy princess up the staircase to my perfectly preserved bedroom. When he lays me down on the bed and climbs on top of me, I forget my worries and think about nothing but him.

18

Ty and I both wake to the sound of shouting in the hallway.

"Fuck you!" Jade screams at the top of her lungs. I know it's her because I was often on the receiving end of her fits. When Jade gets really, really ticked off, her voice cracks and gets brittle like she's not only a chain smoker but also a hundred years old.

"I am not having this conversation with you." Beth.

"Yeah? Well, what's new? You never have conversations with me, Beth. You tell me what to do, chastise me, talk down to me, but you don't ever just *ask* me what I'm doing or why. I'm twenty years old, and I don't need your permission to do a damn thing."

"Okay," Beth says and I can hear her hands hitting her thighs with a slap. I only know because that's a habit of hers when she's stressed. "Okay then, you pay your share of the bills, buy your own food, your own clothes, and then you make all your own decisions. How does that sound?"

"Are you being a mega bitch because Danny's coming over later or because Never is back? Which is it?" I try not to listen, really, because I have this terrible gut feeling that Jade is, at some point, going to say something horrible to me or about me. Granted, I'm willing to cut her some extra slack after what I found out last night, but I think my heart's had about all it can take. My mother has cut into me deep enough to kill, and I have this horrible suspicion that without Ty, I would've done something so disgusting last night that I'd have never recovered.

"You need to learn some tact, Jade. How long are you going to sit around here feeling sorry for yourself? Hmm? Because I, for one, am sick and fucking tired of it. Get a life, Jade, and stop insulting other people about theirs." Footsteps smash across the ground and my door rattles as Jade throws it open and lets it slam into the wall next to her.

"Good morning to you, too," I say, convinced that after five years I should be getting something better for breakfast, maybe some pancakes with smiley faces or something, but no, no my family doesn't work like that. We're such a fucking breeding ground for drama that it makes me ill.

"Have fun digging into my private business last night," Jade says, and I have to blink several times before I can actually register what she's saying.

"Huh?"

"Yeah, Mom told me you were asking about shit that's none of your concern."

"Jade," Beth says, coming up behind my younger sister and trying to touch her shoulder. Jade shrugs it off. I look at her and wonder what the hell I'm going to do because she is a mess. She looks like a deranged biker chick in her black miniskirt, leather jacket, and mask of makeup. Jade is desperate for attention, but she's looking in all the wrong places. "Honey, you have no room to talk. You're always sticking your nose into everyone else's business." Jade ignores her and focuses her rage on me. Always on me. Even after all these years.

"You must have a lot of pent up anger," I tell her as I sit up and try not to notice Ty's beautiful, bare chest and soft, sleepy face. It's been a long time since I've seen a man like that, and I have to say, there's this sort of magic about it, knowing that he's at his most vulnerable by my side. I sort of love it. "To want to rail on me already." Jade flips me off.

"Don't look for Luis, Never," she says venomously. "If you do, I won't ever forgive you." And then she turns away and storms down the stairs to God only knows where. I look at Beth who, despite everything, smiles back at me.

"I'm sorry," she tells me and looks like she wants to come in and sit on the edge of the bed. Her eyes, however, wander over to the lump that is Ty and pause there. "I'll tell you everything later, when she goes out." I nod and am glad that at least there's a few people in this house that are willing to tell me what's gone on, what's *going* on. "And Never," she says as she puts her hand on the doorknob. "I am so glad you're here." Beth blows me a kiss and closes the door.

"I see the spicy streak is a family trait," Ty mumbles, eyes still closed, lip ring bright and shiny in the morning light. I bend down and take it between my teeth, tugging on it until Ty reaches up, tangles his fingers in my hair and kisses me. "Is acidic tongue a dominant gene?" I lean back and slap him lightly with the back of my hand. He gazes up at me and there's this moment where I can imagine a future with him in my mind's eye. It's so bright and perfect that I have to shake my head to get rid of the image. "Something wrong?" he asks me, all mussy and cute with his dark hair sticking up every which way. I close my eyes and shake my head, hoping that what I'm going to say next isn't going to destroy the sweet smile that's on his sexy lips.

"You and I, we're going out with Noah today." I don't mince my words, just get them out before I can second guess myself. After all, Noah is picking us up at two. I don't know what time it is now, but I can't take the chance that Noah will show up before Ty knows. I have a feeling that would be disastrous.

"Where are we going?" he asks which seems like a strange question. He doesn't even sound pissed. I open my eyes and look at him, but he's just yawning and stretching and scratching his taut, sexy belly with his ringed fingers.

"You're not mad?" I ask, and Ty laughs, just up and freaking laughs at me. "Glad I could make your morning," I say and then cringe. Sometimes I'm so mean … I can see what Ty means about this attitude running in the family.

"Nope," he says as he swings his feet out of bed and looks over his shoulder at me. "I want to meet this guy." Ty stands up, and I can't help but check out his ass as he moves around the bed and starts to dig through his suitcase for clothes. *He could be yours,* my mind whispers. *All yours. You can have him completely and wholly if you want, Never. The invitation is there. You have but to accept it.* I swallow and avert my eyes.

"Why?" Ty doesn't answer for awhile, so I turn my attention back to him and watch as he slips on a T-shirt first then a pair of jeans (with no underwear, of course), and turns to face me.

"Because," he tells me, and his voice, although firm, doesn't have the slightest hint of anger in it. "I want to know what he has that I don't." I stare at Ty McCabe for awhile, and he stares back at me, but I don't see any bitterness in his expression, don't hear any in his voice. This makes me feel twice as guilty. I look down at the blankets and curl them into my fist.

"How do you know he does?" I ask, but I don't look up, not until I hear a gentle jingling that draws my eyes to McCabe's wrist. He's switching out his silver bangles for some black ones with red stones. This is a ritual I have never before witnessed firsthand, and there's something about it that makes my heart pump faster and my cheeks heat. Watching Ty slip those bracelets over his hands is erotic somehow. Maybe it's the way his hand slips inside the metal ring, the way his fingers brush the metal oh so gently, I don't know. I decide not to analyze my feelings – there will be plenty of time for that later – and crawl out of bed. Ty's eyes follow me as I kneel down and unzip my bag. "Don't look at me like that," I say and he laughs.

"Yeah, right, Never." Ty bends down, so that we're at eye level with one another. "You're the most beautiful fucking girl I've ever seen, and I can't look? I don't think so." He winks at me, kisses my cheek and leaves me in the bedroom alone, just walks into the hallway by himself and closes the door.

Oh my dear God, Ty fucking McCabe, what am I going to do with you?

I dress myself in some light blue jeans, a red sweater over a black tank, and slip into a pair of black Converse that have been sitting stagnant in this bedroom for five, long years. Wearing them is so strange; walking in them is even stranger. There are certain images in life that get caught in your head, that play like they're on some kind of movie loop. That's how it is with these shoes. I have these pictures in my head of them moving down the hallway at school, of traversing dirt paths ahead of Noah Scott, of walking through the fields with my sisters. I can just look down, see the white toes of these shoes and become Never Regali again. It's so weird that when I open the door to the hallway, I turn around and go back, take the shoes off and slip on some white Nikes.

Ty is leaning against the wall in the kitchen looking like some sort of sex god with a piece of toast hanging from his mouth and a pair of girls hanging from his leg. Darla and Maple are attached to Ty like magnets, talking and babbling together while he nods and pretends he understands what they're saying. Beth is cooking an omelet – presumably for Ty since she's asking him if he wants ham in it – and India is sitting at the table with Lettie and Lorri, coloring a jumbo sized *Welcome Home, Never* card.

"Hey!" India shouts, standing up when I come in. I try to give Ty an *I'm so sorry* look, but he just smiles back at me and doesn't appear to be bothered by the chaos. I'm kind of figuring out that it's hard to ruffle Ty McCabe. He doesn't give a shit about what anybody thinks. Except maybe me. "We've been waiting for you to get up. Don't you know that Noah's going to be here in a half hour?"

"Huh?" I ask, wondering how my sister knows that I have plans with my high school sweetheart.

"Noah called me and asked if we wanted to go," India says brightly, shaking her phone at me. Ty is watching this exchange with interest, sliding his dark eyes between me and my sister. Jade is nowhere to be seen and, of course, neither is my mother. "Oh!" India continues as if her previous statement wasn't weird enough. "And Zella called, too. When I told her you were here, she said she'd changed her mind about staying in Texas for break. So I guess she's coming home for Christmas, too." My heart starts to pump faster. Zella is coming all the way from Texas to see me? Just for me? Is that good or bad? I step into the kitchen and ruffle Lorri's hair. She gazes up at me like I'm some sort of Goddess or something which, of course, makes me feel like complete shit. *Sorry, I ran out on you,* I think silently. *So sorry I left you when you did nothing wrong.*

"How does Noah have your number?" I ask India and the kitchen goes silent. Beth turns her attention to the stove and clears her throat.

"We've been in touch with Noah," she says as she lifts the omelet onto a plate and hands it to India who then passes it to Ty.

"Thank you, beautiful," he says, and I have to keep my lips clamped shut to hold back a stupid comment. Ty McCabe is used to flirting with women. I don't think he even knows when he's doing it anymore. Still, I can see that he doesn't have eyes for my sister, not at all. India blushes anyway and surprisingly, so does Beth.

"In touch with Noah?" I ask, completely and utterly confused. "What? Why?" Why my family should maintain contact with my high school boyfriend seems strange to me. Beth looks at India who looks at everything but me.

"Later," Beth says and then spins around with a big smile on her face. She looks a lot like a copper haired Barbie this morning with her white-white teeth and her apron and her high heels. "I was thinking that you, me, India and Jade could go to dinner together?" She doesn't mention Mom. Nobody mentions Mom. I think it's that moment where I'm looking at Beth and she's smiling back at me that I realize that I'm not going to be able to forgive my mother. Not ever. Not even if she comes crawling to me and says the things she needs to say. And to be honest, I don't think she'll ever do it anyway. I decide then and there that my goal is not to forgive her, but to forget her. I have to cut the emotional strings she has wrapped around my neck. It isn't an easy decision to make; I can feel the pain of it from my head down to my toes. "You look a little pale," Beth says. "Are you alright?" I can't speak, but I nod, and I watch my big sister's face and I know without a doubt that although the woman who gave birth to me is not a mother, I still have one. Beth. Beth is my mother in spirit, and that's okay.

I force a smile to my face.

"As long as Ty's okay with staying here?" I say, asking what I didn't ask last night when I ran off with Noah Scott. He winks at me with a bit of omelet in his mouth and nods.

"Have fun," he says simply and that's that. Is he really that simple? But no, not my Ty, not my bloody, blackhearted Tyson McCabe. He's more complicated than I'll ever be.

"I want to go!" Lettie says, and I can see that at thirteen, she's desperate to make that jump between girl and woman, stumble over to the other side and join us. Beth shakes her head no.

"Sorry honey," she tells my little sister who pouts and crosses her arms over chest, revealing the fact that she is, indeed, still a child. "We have some private stuff to talk about." Beth sighs. "I wish Zella was here now, but we'll just have to make do." I lean down and put my arms around Lettie's shoulders and hug her tight. Thankfully, she hugs me back.

"We'll do something special tomorrow," I whisper to her.

"Maybe a barbeque at the lake or something?" Lettie nods enthusiastically, and I stand up just in time to see Noah's car pull up in front of the house. Immediately, my palms start to sweat and my head feels like it's going to drift into the sky and disappear. Ty senses the shift in my attitude immediately, and I have to keep my gaze off of his. I'm afraid if he sees me, he'll see straight through, and he'll know.

Ty will know that I'm trying to choose between him and Noah, and he won't be happy about it. Not one little bit.

19

Noah Scott walks in the front door dressed in black jeans and a skintight white tee that is deliciously see-through. He doesn't knock, just comes in with a smile on his face and a dog at his heels.

"Never!" Lettie shouts, giving me the distinct impression that she's met the dog-me before. My sisters, including little Darla and Maple, scramble over and throw themselves on the dog who, despite Noah's testimony to the contrary, does not bite. She just sits down and looks resigned to her fate. She's a pretty dog, mind you, but I'm still in the market for that alley tramp.

"Good morning," he says, nodding at Beth, India, me ... pausing on Ty, freezing on Ty, *panicking* at Ty. "Um?" This word slips out of his mouth and just sits there above the table written in bloody ink. Crap.

"Good morning," I say, but Ty beats me to the punch.

"Hey there," he says, setting his plate down on the table and extending his hand, his ringed hand, out to Noah to shake. "Ty McCabe. You must be the infamous Noah Scott."

"Oh, I don't know about the infamous part, but yeah, I'm Noah." The two men shake hands, and I swear to God, I will testify to this, that there is a spark in that kitchen. Heat explodes from the two of them and hits me right in the chest. Fuck. Fuck. Fuck. "Um, sorry," Noah continues as he withdraws his hand and tries to catch my eyes. I look away purposely. "I'm sorry. I didn't know Never had brought a ... " Everyone waits anxiously for me to fill in the missing word. It's like the world's most horrible game of Mad Libs, one where nobody wins.

"I have no family, so Never offered to let me come with her for the holidays," Ty says, reminding me that in less than three weeks, it will be Christmas. This house has no lights, no tree, no presents. I make a promise to myself that I'll ask Beth about it later. He also leaves his position in my life purposely vague, but why? Ty says that I'm his, that I belong to him, so why is he just laying by the wayside and letting me fumble through this? If our positions were switched, I'd be clawing Noah Scott's eyes outs. *So just pick Ty already,* my damaged heart commands me. I ignore it which is probably stupid, and try to smile. It sort of hurts my face. I haven't smiled, really truly smiled, in a good long while. *Except, of course, when you're with Ty. Idiot.*

"So, big family trip to the river?" I say and honestly, it sort of sounds like hell. "I'm gonna go have a cigarette." I touch my back pockets but can't find anything.

"I've got what you're looking for, baby," Ty says, and I think I actually pass out standing up. I come to quick and keep my eyes off of Noah's face.

"Yeah, alright," I say as I grab Ty's hand and drag him outside and around the back of the barn. When Lettie and Lorri try to follow, I tell them I don't want to see them dead from second hand smoke and buy myself a small slice of alone time with Ty. It's going to be a long day. I don't wait for Ty to hand me a cig and reach my hand down his back pocket to grab the box. Admittedly his ass feels damn good, nice and firm and fucking sexy as hell. He raises his eyebrows at me, but doesn't say a thing.

"Got a light?" I ask as I stick a Marlboro Red between my lips and pass the box back to him. Ty puts one in his mouth and leans forward so that the cigarettes are touching before he lights us up together. I watch his dark eyes the whole time, certain that he's going to say something about Noah. He doesn't.

"I have to say," he tells me with a wicked grin. "That I fucking love this tractor."

"Ty McCabe," I snap and then sigh, blowing smoke out between my lips. "Well?" He looks at me like he doesn't know what I'm talking about and continues to smoke, one hand in his front pocket, nice and casual like. "Noah," I say finally. "Noah Scott. What do you think?" Ty looks at me like I'm the world's biggest idiot and throws his cigarette to the ground before he starts to walk away. I stamp on it to put it out, convinced that Ty better get used to putting them out on his own. It's not damp here like it is back … home. Cigarettes cause fires real fast here. I stumble after Ty and grab his arm. He spins to face me with a pinched mouth. "What did I do?" I ask, and Ty rolls his eyes before going for another cigarette, a Djarum Black this time.

"Never, seriously?" he says as he follows me back towards the tractor. I lean against the tire and remember the tears I shed last night, the things I said to him. I'm such a fucking idiot; I hate myself sometimes.

"What?"

"You asked me what I think about Noah Scott?" Ty laughs. "Oh, yeah," he says around his cig. "Your boyfriend's real fuckin' nice. What a cutie. I heart the fuck out of him. What a catch." I take the cigarette from my mouth and throw it at Ty. It doesn't come even close to hitting him. He snuffs it out with his boot. "Honestly? I want to smash his face in. Is that what you want to hear?" I cross my arms over my chest.

"I don't know, Ty. Jesus Christ, I wasn't asking you for dating advice."

"What were you asking me then?" he says and then sighs. I watch as Ty wraps this awesome self-control around himself. It's almost a physical change, very impressive, something I could never do. "Look, it doesn't matter. I'm mildly okay with this, alright? I mean, if you choose me because I tie you up in the bedroom and forbid you to see him, what good does that do me?" Ty pauses. "Though I'm not opposed to doing that if you're interested."

"Ty," I say, leveling a look on him. If he's going to freak out and run off, fuck some bitch behind my back, I want to know now.

"I want you to choose me for me," Ty says and my heart turns to slush in my chest. "I want you to say fuck Noah Scott and mean it. When you can do that, really do that, come tell me. It'll happen, I know it will."

"I want to ask you a question," I say, and I can't help but move forward and put my arms around Ty's waist. He's so fucking dark and beautiful and twisted and perfect. I can't keep my hands off of him. He is also officially now the only man I have had sex with more than once which I think is pretty cool but which I keep to myself.

"Ask away," he says and then smiles meanly when I look up at him. "But I may choose to take the fifth."

"Are you going to spook?" I ask him, heart fluttering like a butterfly. *Trapped, trapped, she's trapped until you let her go. If she comes back, only then can you be convinced of her love.* "Are you going to … " I choke on my heart and have to swallow her back down. "Are you going to run off and fuck somebody?" Ty grabs my chin roughly, maybe a little too roughly, but his pain is so evident in his fingertips that I forgive him.

"I will never, ever hurt you like that again," he says fiercely. "We promised to be honest with each other, so let's be honest. I won't touch another woman, maybe as long as I live. I can't stop thinking about you, hurting for you." Ty kisses me hard with his teeth and pulls back, smoke drifting from his mouth into my own as I breathe. "Now tell me, are you going to fuck Noah Scott?" I shake my head and then pause.

"Not without telling you first," I whisper, and I hate myself for saying that. Why can't I just run off with Ty McCabe and live happily ever after? I know why, though. I know that if I do that, I'll have what-ifs following me forever. I have to banish them, all of them. I have to reconnect with my sisters, save Jade, snip my mother from my soul, and I have to find Luis and confront him. I have to do all of this to move on, and I have to understand my feelings for Noah.

"Thanks for telling me the truth," Ty whispers and in his

eyes I see that he's glad, truly, even if the words are not what he wants to hear. "Now, let's go get some quality time in with your boyfriend."

20

"So, Ty, um, is that short for Tyler?" Noah asks during *the* most uncomfortable drive of my entire life. We're sitting in Noah's car, and by we I mean me, Ty, Noah, and India. It's kind of ... shitty.

"Nope," Ty says and rolls his window down to smoke. Noah cringes, but Ty either doesn't notice or doesn't give a shit. I'm going with the latter. "Tyson." He pauses. "If you call me that though, I'm gonna get kinda pissed off." I think about jumping out the window and dying on the highway. Maybe that would be better than this? Maybe not.

"Tyson McCabe," India repeats and Ty laughs. He's not about to get pissed off at pretty, little India. "That's a nice name. You don't like it?"

"I like Ty better," he says, and that's it. The conversation dies before it even really gets started. I stroke Never's fur gently and try not to think about that poetry class where the professor likened petting a dog to stroking a woman's vagina. *I wish I were a lesbian. Men suck.*

"So, Noah," Ty says, sounding kind of ... bitchy. I reach up from around the back of his seat and tug on his eyebrow ring. He grabs my wrist and presses a nasty kiss to the back of my hand that *everyone* notices. "This is a really nice car. You must have a great job." Noah scratches the back of his head and isn't sure what to say.

"His dad got it for him," I insert, trying to distract them both. India's been staring at me like I'm a ghost for the last ten minutes, so I try to steer the conversation over to her, so we can get to know each other better. After all, that's what I'm here for. These ... boys? men? ... whatever are taking over my everything, and I don't know how to react to it. A few months back, I was so alone in the world, I might've ended my own life had things not changed. And then I met Ty in a bar and so now everything is different, and I just owe him the fucking world ... Why can't I just tell Noah Scott to fuck off? "So, India," I begin, putting my hands on my knees and a fake smile on my face. "How's school going?" India shrugs and licks the side of her mouth, a nervous gesture I remember well. I've always had that, at least, a good memory. Without memories, I'd be nothing but ash.

"It's okay," she says with a sigh, and I can tell there's something bothering her, something that she wants to tell me but not Noah or Ty. I reach out and touch her hand, let her wrap her fingers around mine and let it go for now. Sometime later, I'll find the time to talk privately with her, with them all. I'll say my 'sorry's and hopefully hear some of theirs; I'll see who they've become and who they want to be. Maybe everything really will be alright in the end? "I kind of want to drop out," India blurts suddenly.

"No." I say it quickly and calmly, but firmly. She stares at me like I'm a crazy person, like she thought I was the last person in the world that would tell her *no*.

"Listen," Ty says as he turns around and smiles back at my sister with his best bad boy smile. It works and I can see that she is riveted on anything he might say. For better or worse, Ty McCabe has India Regali's full, undivided attention. "You don't have to go to school. If you don't want to be there, then it's pointless, a waste of fucking time, but," he says before either Noah or I can jump down his throat. "You better have a backup plan, something airtight, otherwise you'll end up on the street corner giving ten dollar blow jobs." India stares back at him with big, wide eyes and Noah coughs to clear his throat.

"I don't think – " Noah begins.

Ty cuts him off with a wave of his ringed hand. The jingling bangles stop Noah mid-sentence. "Quiet blondie, I've been there, done that, so I know what I'm talking about." Ty pauses, and I avoid Noah's eyes in the rearview mirror. He wants to know who Ty is, obviously, but what can I say now? I'll have to try to get a moment alone with him at the river. On second thought … I see that Ty is staring straight at me, burning me up with his gaze, the curve of his lips. My chest relaxes and I have to fight the urge to sigh. Me. Sigh. Over a guy. Fucking weird. "Tell me, India, what do you do? What makes you, you?"

She answers without hesitation. "Music."

Ty winks at her and turns back around, lacing his fingers behind his head.

"Then you're set," he says and pauses. "Provided you can actually play … "

"Sing," India says with a smile. "I can sing."

"Ah, I have to hear it to believe it," Ty says and India *giggles*. It's not intentional, it's just that Ty makes women feel wanted. A trick of the trade, I guess.

"Here we are," Noah says, sounding terribly relieved. The river, known simply as 'Hatchett's' is a winding, sweeping monster of powerful currents and white froth that hides the river's sharp teeth from the viewers above. I've seen more than one brave adventurer torn apart on those rocks, some of whom made it, and others …

"Fucking gorgeous," Ty says, leaning forward over the dash. "Shit and fuck." Noah cringes, but India barely notices Ty's language. It's sort of a … *thing* … in our family. Beth is already waiting in the parking lot. I have to say that even though she now drives a minivan, she's still like a bat outta hell when she hits the road. Darla and Maple are playing in the grass with Lettie and Lorri while Jade sulks in the shade nearby like a vampire. Her skin is pale and stretched taut across her face like she hasn't been sleeping much lately. I need to talk to her soon, before she becomes a Mini-Me and spirals straight into hell. Jade couldn't take what I've been through; she would die.

Noah parks next to my sister's van and we all climb out into the cool, dry air of winter. It has this bite to it, something that tells me that a storm is on the way, but for now, the sun is shining weakly above the trees and everything is peaceful. Things can change real fast around here; I only hope Ty and I don't get stuck in a cellar with my family. Tornadoes are not exactly my thing.

"Never, look," Lorri says, racing up to me with a daisy chain clutched in her hand. I smile and bend down, letting her lay it across my hair. As she does this, she points at my scalp. "Your hair is changing color." Roots. She's talking about my roots. There's going to be a time here soon where I'll have to decide if I'm keeping the black and red, going back to the copper, or changing it up all together. Maybe I should be a blonde? I wonder if Ty likes blondes. I don't wonder about Noah. What does that say?

"Just as pretty as when you left," Noah says as he glances first at the river and then at me. The reference isn't lost on me. Not Ty either.

"Just as fucking beautiful," he says even though he's never seen this place before in his life. Or has he? Fuck. How would I know? I have no idea where Ty comes from. He doesn't have any discernible accent that I can place (not to me anyway), and he hasn't mentioned anything that might give him away. I stare at Ty McCabe for a moment, and he stares back at me. "See something you like?" he asks which makes me roll my eyes and take Lorri's hand. We head over to the grassy area that fronts the head of the trail here, and I do my best to smile at Jade. I sort of want to yell at her to get her friggin' head on straight, but what good would that do me? Jade is just like me: she's confrontational and she doesn't play well with others.

"You must be one tough bitch to hike in those boots," I joke, but my words fall flat. Jade scowls at me.

"Fuck off, Never."

"Jesus Christ, Jade," Beth says in her best mom voice. It's pretty good, even better than it was when I left. Guess having a kid really refined Beth's best skills. "Can you be pleasant for thirty seconds? That would be a God given gift."

"Why are we even here anyway?" Jade complains as she

stands up and I see that her skirt is even shorter than the ones I'm used to wearing. I say nothing. "So Never can pretend she's part of the family?"

"She *is* part of the family," Beth says and her tone is not pleasant, like it's been poured from iron or something. My sister tucks her short hair behind her ear and it immediately escapes, brushing against her cheek as she bends down and picks up her daughter. Jade glares daggers at me, further separating us, further alienating me from any chance of feeling like I actually belong here.

"Look," I say because I'm starting to hurt. When I hurt, I get pissed. When I get pissed, I kick ass. "I don't know what your problem is with me. If anything, you owe *me* an apology, but if you want to just call it even and drop all of this crap, then let's do it." Jade steps back and raises her eyebrows like *What the fuck, sister?*

"Who the hell do you think you are?" she screeches, not holding back even an ounce of her rage. "You don't know me. You don't know this family or what you put us through. You are the world's most selfish human being, Never *Regali*." I don't correct her. What good will that do? I just stand there with Noah on one side of me and Ty on the other. Both are silent. Both know that I have to handle this on my own.

"That isn't true," I tell her, trying to keep my voice soft. Maple is starting to cry. I don't want her to associate pain or tears with me. What kind of a fresh start is that? "I have thought about you every single day for the past five years and I – "

"You're a nasty, filthy fucking whore, Never," Jade growls as Beth hands Maple to India who takes my three youngest sisters away from this fight and over to a small play area at the end of the parking lot. "I know everything. Everything. We all do." I stare at her because I'm not sure what she's talking about. How could they know? Who could've told them? I look over at Ty, and he shakes his head slightly. *No.* Anyway, he would never do that to me. Ty isn't like that. "You're a disgusting, diseased, useless woman. A throw away." I take deep breaths; I push my feelings back; I die a little inside.

"And you're a spoiled rotten, foulmouthed little witch." My eyes snap over to Ty. He doesn't move forward, doesn't raise his voice, doesn't even look angry. He just says what he says and means every word of it. "I don't know what you think you know or how you know it, but I don't give a shit. You need to take a step back and examine your own life before you start judging hers because to me, Never is perfect."

Oh.

My heart cracks in two as I glance over at Ty and realize for the first time that maybe this whole thing isn't about deciding whether Noah is good enough or whether I love him. This is about deciding that Ty is better, that I love him more, that I can't live without him. I gasp and turn around, rest my hands on my sister's van, try to breathe.

"Are you alright?" Noah asks, obviously a bit out of the loop. I don't fill him in; I *can't* fill him in and have him look at me like I'm someone else. At least in Noah's eyes, there is no taint, no blood, no sign that he knows what I've done or where I've been.

"Fine," I say as a dizzy spell takes over me, and I find myself sitting down with my head against the tire. I don't know if it's nerves or angst or anxiety or what, but I can't stand up, not yet. "Just peachy."

I crack open my eyes for a moment and the world spins. Ty is walking away with Jade and Noah is sitting next to me, rubbing his thumb over my knuckles. Beth is standing dumbstruck in the same place she's been this whole time. When she turns and faces me, her face falls and she starts to get teary eyed.

"Never, I'm sorry," she whispers as she comes over and sits down, too. "I don't know what's wrong with her. She's just like this all the time now." I sit up and try to swallow. It takes me three tries. I look for a cigarette and practically have a panic attack when I can't find one. I'm so used to being around Ty that he carries them for both us. *Ty.* Beth pulls a box out of her purse and hands me one. It's a freaking Newport, but I take it anyway and let her light me up.

"What did she tell you?" I ask my sister, meeting her eyes, trying to gauge the truth in her next words. "What do you know?" Beth stares back at me, and it's that little second of silence that tells me she doesn't know anything. And neither does Jade. She was calling me names, calling me on something else, too, maybe, but not the truth. She was making horrible generalizations, guessing, grabbing at straws, and the worst part is that she was right. She was fucking right.

"I don't know what you're talking about," Beth says with a sigh, and I can see that I've unwittingly revealed to her that I've got a secret. A big, fat, nasty, bloody secret. "Please don't be angry with her," my sister pleads and little lines of worry pop up all over her young face. This isn't fair to her. Nothing is fair. The world isn't fair. I hate this kind of shit.

"Okay," I whisper because I don't have the strength to cut two people off of my heart. If I do, I'll bleed to death. My mom, she isn't going to change, but Jade ... she's flippant and angry and full of hate, but she isn't numb. Numb is so much worse. I look over at Noah who takes my hand and puts it to his lips, presses the most gentle kiss across my knuckles. He's this little blip of color in all of this black and white.

I glance up and can't find Ty or Jade. I'll have to trust that he knows what he's doing. He's good with broken people, Ty is.

"I guess our hike is ruined?" I say as Noah's dog, Never, starts to bark from the area of the play structure. Beth says nothing but gets up to check. Noah, he stays.

"I don't see why it has to be," he tells me as he brushes some hair from my face. "If you want, you and I could take a short walk together." He pauses. "Alone." I look up and try to find Ty one more time before I give him my answer.

"Okay," I say with a sad smile. "Okay, I'd like that."

21

Ty and Jade are waiting for Noah and me when we get back, lying on their backs in the grass beneath a massive oak tree. They're not touching, not even close, but Jade scrambles to her feet when she sees us come around the small fence with the bitch-Never by our sides. She yaps at Jade and then starts sniffing around Ty's crotch. He lays there and doesn't move. I have this really disturbing fear that Ty has slept with Jade, but then, maybe he thinks I slept with Noah. We're just going to have to trust each other this time. It's going to be hard, but it has to be done. There's no other way.

"Beth, um, took everyone else home," Jade whispers and I can see that most of her makeup is gone. She must've cleaned it off while I was walking the winding river banks with Noah and discussing birds. And cars. And vacation destinations. He didn't ask about my secret, even though I could see that he knew, too. They'll all know now, but I may not tell any of them. I have to see how things go. I let Noah hold my hand but only for a little while then I pretended to be more interested in throwing sticks and stuff for Never to chase. I don't want Noah to think we're dating again because we're not. We're just, I don't know, testing the waters or something. "Never," Jade begins with a big breath and I fear that Ty has told her everything, spilled my dark secrets for her to see. I tense up and can practically feel Noah's pretty eyes trying to pick me apart. "I'm sorry, but I need you to be sorry, too." Jade gets tears in her eyes. Mine remain dry, for the moment anyway. "I'm sorry I didn't believe you about Luis, but I'm also mad that you didn't stick around and stand up for me. I wanted you to be there, Never, I really did." Jade pauses and looks at Noah like he's intruding. He gets it pretty quick and moves away ... towards Ty. Nice. I hope they have a really fun conversation about me behind my back. Or in front of it. Whatever. "So please, tell me your story." I blink several times to try to understand what she's just said.

"Oh." I look over at Ty who I can hear is speaking to Noah but over the roar of water, can't make out the words. *He didn't tell her.* I look Jade in the face, search her for a moment and see nothing but pain and angst. She's just sad, just a lost soul, not a broken one. I hold out my arms and she steps into them, lets me hold her tight for just a moment, just one blissful, perfect moment.

"I love you," Jade says to me and changes my world without even knowing it. Tears come then, finally, like a waterfall, they cascade down my cheeks and drip onto my sweater. Jade has them, too, and we both look at one another with pouty lips for a moment before we burst into laughter. The boys glance back at us, but they both know better than to interfere. This is sister stuff. You don't mess with sister stuff. Especially if you have a penis.

"I'm sorry," I tell Jade, and I mean it. I really, truly do. She nods her head, and I know that although things can't be fixed so easily, that there's at least a foundation laid for us to build on. Because of Ty. It has to be because of Ty. What he said to her, I don't know, but it was something special. "We'll go out for ice cream," I say as I take a deep breath. "And I'll tell you what I can. I can't promise that it'll be everything, but it will be something." Jade understands this and nods.

"Okay," she begins and then pauses like she wants to say something. I notice how much prettier she looks without her makeup, how much younger. I like her so much better this way. "Ty," she begins, her voice low enough that I know the boys can't hear. "He's pretty cool." And then she's turning away and grabbing Never by the collar before she can dart out in front of a pickup truck.

I walk over to Ty and stand above him, noticing that his eyes are cracked open and he's got a cigarette in his mouth. He looks so fucking gorgeous stretched out on the grass like that, long and lean and hard. I want to straddle him, fuck the shit out of him right then and there. My thighs clench tightly and I have to look away to stop my heart from galloping away from me.

"Have a good walk, Nev?" he asks, and he doesn't sound pissy, just curious.

"Yes," I say as I resist the urge to lie down next to him and curl myself against his side, feel his ringed fingers in my hair, his mouth on mine. "You?" Ty takes the cigarette out of his mouth and sits up.

"Jade and I had a nice talk. I think it was helpful. I've kind of decided that I want to counsel people, like teens or something, you know? People with problems. I think that's my life calling." I don't say anything because Noah is scrutinizing this conversation, and I just don't feel like talking in front of him. "Seriously, baby, I think this could be the start of a beautiful future." *Together* hangs in the air after his words as he stands up and gives me a smoky kiss smack dab on the lips. Noah watches silently, and when Ty walks away, he grabs my arm. He unlocks the car with his key fob so Ty, bitch-Never, and Jade can climb in giving us a second of privacy.

"Who is this guy, Never?" Noah asks and in his words, there's a judgment. He doesn't like Ty. Now, whether it's because he's just jealous or because he senses something in him, I don't know, but what I do know is that if Noah doesn't like Ty, he doesn't like me because we're the same, him and me. Ty and I are two halves of a whole. It's just a fact, a plain and simple fact.

"He's my ... " It takes me the longest moment in history to answer this question. "He's my soul mate."

22

Noah takes us all back to the house and stays. My soul mate comment actually seems to invigorate rather than discourage him from seeking my affection. We play games and he sits really, really close to me, laughs loudest at my jokes, touches me gently. Ty watches and says nothing, sits across the room from me, frowns with an unlit cigarette in his mouth, and makes my little sisters giddy with joy when he agrees to play dress up with them.

When it gets dark, Noah goes to leave and there's this awkward moment where we don't know what we're supposed to do – kiss? hug? shake hands? – so we do nothing and it's one of the tensest moments of my life.

"See you soon, I hope," he whispers as he disappears out the door and Ty drapes himself over my shoulders. He's wearing a sparkly tiara and a pink dress that my sisters have cut up for their fashion show. It hangs in rags from his strong shoulders, bares his belly beneath. I want to grab his hand, drag him upstairs, and explore his body, but I can't. It's almost time for *dinner*. The dinner where I'm supposed to find out everything about Jade and Luis and whatever else happened while I was gone. I've already met Danny, Maple's father, and that was bad enough. He was an uptight, suit wearing piece of shit who could not have looked any less thrilled to be picking up his child for the night. Guess my sister was good enough to fuck but not worth enough to be pleasant to. He didn't even say *hello* to her.

"Thank God," Ty whispers, breath hot as hell against my ear. "I thought he was never going to leave." I try to pry him off of me, but instead, he spins me around and keeps hold of my wrist, places his other hand against my lower back and kisses me half to death. Ty's lips are hungry and his teeth are needy, biting and eating away at me while I do my best to keep from moaning and collapsing on the floor in a puddle.

"*Never*," Beth hisses from the staircase, causing Ty to step back with the world's phoniest *Who me?* look on his pretty face. Guess his charm works on women of all walks because my sister smiles coquettishly and reprimands only me. "There are children in this house."

"Yeah, okay," I tell her, admiring the white dress she's put on for our outing. Beth looks so pretty and grown up; I wonder when I'll look like that, if I'll ever look like that. Maybe it's because she had a baby? I don't know, but I'm not having one anytime soon. I remind myself to pick up condoms while I'm out tonight, whether I want to use them or not. When we go back to California, I'll get some more birth control pills from the clinic. For now, I have to be smart. Ty is a stud, and I have no doubt that he could get me pregnant with a mere glance.

"Get dressed," Beth commands, assuming I brought something more appropriate for the snooty restaurant we're driving almost an hour to get to. They have seven items on their menu. Seven. And they're all over thirty bucks a plate. I wonder who's going to pay for it. I imagine the clothing in my suitcase and know that what I'm wearing is probably the nicest, most conservative thing I have.

"I think I'll just wear this," I say, and she rolls her eyes at me. It feels good, actually, to have Beth look at me like I'm just another sister. I sort of love it.

"Suit yourself," she says, flipping her short hair and yelling over her shoulder. "India, hurry up, we haven't got all night."

"Hey," Ty whispers to me and reaches into his back pocket. He pulls out a wad of cash and hands it to me. I stare at it and can't help but wonder where it came from. If it's money from his whoring, I don't want it, and not because I blame him for what he did or because I'm judging him but just because I'm jealous. He senses this and smiles softly.

"My last paycheck from the store," he tells me. "The grocery store." Ty reaches out and curls my fingers around the money. There's at least a hundred bucks there, conservatively. "Maybe you can grab some stuff for me while you're out?" he says and he's smiling wicked nasty at me. "And pay for dinner, too." I don't want to take Ty's money, but I don't have much of my own left, so I stuff it in the pocket of my jeans.

"Like?"

"Like Magnums, 'kay?" *Guess we're on the same page.* Ty kisses me on the nose which is too fucking cute for a sizzling sex addict like him, and spins away to intercept Darla who's giggling and running with a fairy princess wand in hand. He growls at her and grabs her around the waist, swinging her in a circle like a dancer while she shouts and screams with joy. She likes him far better than she likes me which is okay. It's hard not to like Ty McCabe.

"You can judge a man by how he interacts with children," Beth whispers as she walks by me and into the kitchen. "It's the oldest trick in the book." I roll my eyes. My sister can't help herself. She's kind of old fashioned sometimes. Ty moves into the living room with Lettie and Lorri and Darla, but I don't follow them. I won't go in there, not yet. That's the room where my father took his last breath, and I know that if I set foot in there now, that I'll be bombarded with memories that I really don't want.

"Ready," a voice says from above me, and I glance up to find Jade in a soft, pink dress that flows like silk, hair up in a bun, makeup soft but perfect. Beth.

"She dressed you, didn't she?" I ask and my sister gives me a real smile, so genuine it could knock your socks off.

"She's being nice to you now," Jade tells me as she comes down the stairs and nearly trips on her own shoes. "But just you wait. Once you're absorbed fully into the fold, she'll start in on you."

"Hey," India calls from the top of the stairs. "No complaining." I laugh, can't help it. "Oh shut up, Never," she sighs as she descends the steps like a cloud, all light, white fluff and bows. It's the most deranged piece of fabric I've ever seen. Maybe I wouldn't look like such a tool if I put on my red dress, the one I wore the night I met Ty? A slut maybe, but not a tool.

"Be right back," I say as I go upstairs and throw on my dress, pin my hair up with a clip from my past, and smear on some lipstick. The neckline might be a little low and the hem might be a little high, but as I examine myself in the mirror I can't help but think I look pretty good. Apparently, Beth agrees because she compliments me when I come downstairs, giving my other two sisters something to exchange an eye roll over. When Ty sees me, he smiles softly and pulls some rings off his right hand. He jingles these around in his palm and then tries to pass one to me. It's the gold one with the ruby setting.

"I can't take this," I tell him, my heart threatening to break free from my chest and go skidding across the floor for all my sisters to see. They're watching this exchange with interest, and I can't blame them. I mean, when a guy gives a girl a ring, it usually means something pretty special. Now, Ty might not be asking me to marry him, but he is giving me one of his mother's rings.

"Please," he tells me, leaving his hand suspended in midair. "Don't make me look like an asshat. Take it." I laugh, as do Jade and India behind me, and let Ty press the ring into my hand, curl his fingers around mine, pull me to his lips for a kiss.

"So, are you guys, like, together-together?" India asks as Ty slides his arms around me and just holds us in this space between now and forever, this warm bit of bliss that has no name, that exists solely for the two of us.

Ty doesn't answer. He knows that I have to answer this question, that this is my call to make. I touch his lip ring, slide my fingertips up the side of his face, tug on his nose ring. Ty, the man with the butterfly tattoos and an acidic past that burns hot inside of him, has a hold on me that I can't resist. No matter what I say now, no matter what I do, he knows that. Noah Scott or no, Ty is special, and I would be one, stupid, fucking bitch not to see that.

"Yeah," I say. "Yeah, I guess we are."

23

In the car, I have a hard time joining the conversation, partly because I don't know anything about the pageant that Jade took part in last summer and partly because I have a *boyfriend.* Ty is my boyfriend. Except for Noah, I've never had one of those. I don't know what to do with one. *Love it, keep it, treasure it.* Which brings up another good point. Noah. What do I do with Noah?

"So," I say, interrupting a fest of giggling that sort of makes me feel like an outsider. "How are you guys so close to Noah? I mean, after I left, I can't imagine why you would keep in touch with him." Beth goes silent for a second, and I think she's going to say something like, *Oh, Zella dated him,* or something as equally perturbing as that. The thought makes me jealous whether I want it to or not. All these years, I've always kept Noah in the back of my mind, earmarked as belonging to me, using him to compare any living, breathing man against. And now here I am and he's a possibility, and I can't keep my hands off of Ty McCabe.

"At first, we kept in touch with him just in case one or the other of us heard from you. After awhile, when it was obvious you weren't coming back," Beth chokes on her words and gets tears in her eyes again. Everybody else remains dry eyed. "He just started coming around when we needed him. You know, to babysit or fix something or whatever. And then, um … " Beth pauses, and I can feel that the subject is now out of her control. We're waiting for someone else. We're waiting for Jade.

"He kicked Luis in the balls when he tried to rape me," Jade gushes, and when I look back at her, her face is in her hands. I don't tell her this, but I'm glad that she calls Luis by his name. She knows he's her biological father, but she doesn't call him Dad. "Um, he was drunk off his ass, and he just fucking threw me down. If Noah hadn't walked in … " Jade begins, but she doesn't finish. Nobody elaborates on this story which is fine by me. I know all I need to know.

"I'm a sex addict," I say and the words sound kind of stupid in the darkness of the minivan. Nobody responds for awhile.

"What's … that exactly?" India asks, and I have to remember that she's only sixteen, that she and Jade are virgins. I try to keep to generalizations. My hands are sweaty and shaky, and I wish with all my heart and soul that Ty was here, that I could wrap my fingers around his ringed ones and squeeze.

"I had sex to feel better about myself," I tell her and try not to choke on my own words. My chip earring is still hanging by my cheek, reminding me what I've been through and how lucky I am to be alive.

"How many people?" Jade asks, and I cringe. I don't think she was asking to be mean, just curious, just trying to understand who I am and where I've been, who I've become. She wants to know me which is more than I can say for my mother.

"I don't know," I reply honestly, and that's that. Beth moves on to other things, pointless things like how they had to have the water heater replaced two years back, and how the tree in the back of the house, the one that we use to climb when we were kids, fell down and came *this* close to hitting the house and killing Jade in her sleep. Beth talks briefly, oh so briefly, about how it was to live with Luis. Without actually saying the words, I get her drift: *you were right.* When she's done talking, she pauses and turns on a horrible Christian rock/country radio station that makes me gag. After three songs though, we pull into the parking lot and she shuts off the car.

"Never," she says as she spins to look at me, reaches out and cups my face between her hands. "I am so sorry. I believed you, I did, but I was going through a phase where I wanted Mom to approve of me, and I just – " I cut her off with a smile. She can't know how much her words mean to me. It's just impossible. That simple phrase, that sorry, that tells me that she cares, that she regrets, that she hopes for something better and right now, that's all that matters to me. I open my mouth to speak and then pause. I had been laboring under the assumption that Darla was Luis' biological child, but if he tried to hurt Jade four years ago and got kicked out, and Darla is only three then ...

"Who is Darla's father?" I ask and although it might not be funny to anyone else, it is to us because this is the story of our life, and we're in charge of the punch lines. Beth starts to cry again, but she's laughing at the same time.

"Well," Jade begins, sliding forward in her seat so she can look right at me when she says this. "There was this Def Leppard tribute band that came into town a few years back ..."

24

Dinner with my sisters is ... blissfully normal. I think we're all sort of tired of living in the past, so whether or not we should be discussing past issues doesn't really matter. As soon as we sit in those chairs and pick up those horribly pretentious menus, we can't stop laughing and the world is suddenly this whole new place for me. It's a bit scary. But maybe I'm in a good mood because I've decided what I need to do, what *needs* to be done. When we get home, the house is dark and quiet. I say my good nights and head straight up the stairs, feeling strangely at peace with myself and the decisions I've made. This mood may not last long, but I'm going to ride it for all it's worth.

"Want to do something with me?" I ask Ty as soon as I step into my bedroom and close the door behind me. If Jade finds out what I'm up to, she'll never forgive me. But what she doesn't understand is that I'm not just doing this for her, I'm doing this for me, too. Ty glances up at me, peeling his eyes away from the pages of a blue and yellow notebook. My notebook. My fucking journal. "Um, do you have any fucking sense of privacy or self preservation?" I ask the shirtless hottie who's lying stretched across my bed in a pair of black sweats but nothing else. His skin is bronzed and beautiful, like the surface of a penny, tanned from the sun and absolutely, one hundred percent kissable. I glance away as Ty sets the book beside him.

"Hey," he says, and I can hear the bed creaking as he sits up. "There wasn't much else to do after your little sisters went to bed." He pauses. "Though I did speak with your mother." I glance back at him and am determined not to get lost in the beautiful lines of his body. If I do, I may very well just climb into bed with him and forget this whole thing. But I can't. I can't forget it because it may very well be one of my top five moments in life. I have to confront Luis about my father, about Jade. I have to because if I don't, I will always have this anger inside of myself. The anger that makes me fuck guys I don't love, that brings tears to my eyes when there shouldn't be any. I have to get rid of it, and I need Ty to help me. If Ty doesn't come along with me, I may very well kill that sick son of a bitch.

"Why?" Ty sits up completely and puts his feet on the

floor. I notice that he doesn't release his hold on the notebook.

"She was asking about you."

"And? What did you tell her?" My heart is thumping away like a mad thing, and it isn't only because beautiful, fucking, tortured, twisted Ty McCabe is sitting half-naked in front of me. I have to know what my mother asked about, what she said. I still know that I have to cut her off for my own well being, but that doesn't mean I want to, doesn't mean I'm not curious about her. Somehow, coming from her womb has connected us in a way that nobody else could possibly understand save my sisters. However, this binds me only to them and not to her. I imagine it would be different if she loved me. *If* is a very big word.

"I said you had the greatest capacity for love that I've ever seen in any other human being." I lock my gaze on Ty's and try to tell him how I feel without words. Somehow, he gets it. He always does.

"What else?" Ty shakes his head.

"That's all she wanted to know," he responds honestly. He thinks my feelings will be hurt, and they should be, but they're not. I just nod my head and move on. That's how I have to deal with my mom now, how I should've dealt with her all those years ago. I should've cut her off and tried to make up with everybody else, stuck around, been with Noah. But then … Maybe fate took me on this crazy ride with the very purpose of meeting Ty. Maybe he and I are meant to be together, like some kind of twisted, fucked up fairytale couple from a bloody Grimm story. I glance at the journal. I should be mad that he read it, but somehow, it seems appropriate.

"You have no sense of privacy," I repeat and he grins at me, dimples and all.

"This was a riveting read," he says as he shakes the journal. His bracelets jingle like bells. "I like the part where you write a whole page of *Fuck You's* to the assholes at your school." Ty licks his sexy lips and flips open to a full page of angry black scribbles. "To that fucking, Goddamn, cock sucking little cunt who refused to pass me a tampon when I was in the women's bathroom. I hope you go to hell and die." I laugh because that moment, when it happened, infuriated me to within an inch of my life. Doesn't seem like such a big deal anymore.

"Get up," I tell him as I look longingly at the tiny sprinkle of hair that leads from the bottom of Ty's bellybutton and into his pants. A happy trail, they call that. I've followed many but none as nice as Ty's. None of the bad boys I ever slept with had that smile that burns like the sun, those deep eyes, that perfect body, that … Fuck. To anyone but me, it would sound as if I was head over heels in love. Since I have no way to judge that emotion, I move past it, ignorant and blissfully stupid. One day I'll get it. "Let's burn some memories to ash."

Ty dresses quickly and follows me outside with a fresh pack of cigs tucked in the pocket of his pants and an extra lighter. I dig a small hole in the dirt next to our favorite tractor and start to tear up the pages of my journal. Ty bends down next to me, and we spend these few, perfect quiet moments burning the memories of my high school life to bits of black that float in the gentle breeze. Ty even lights us up with the fire from the cover which I think is pretty fucking special in some kind of strange, screwed up way.

"You know what," Ty tells me as we stand in unison and look at each other. He still doesn't know we're going to see Luis, but I think he senses it. "You really are fucking beautiful." I roll my eyes, but I have to admit, I kind of like it when he says that.

"You're a troll," I tell him as we blow sweet puffs of smoke at one another. It's like we're speaking with our cigarettes, communicating in some strange way that nobody else will ever understand. It's kind of nice.

"Where are we going?" he asks me finally as we both drop our butts to the ground and step on them.

"To find the fucker that killed my father," I say.

No other explanation and Ty just says, "Sounds good to me, baby."

We climb into India's truck and drive down the road to forgiveness, one that's paved with the thick, dark bricks of revenge.

25

I can't stop spinning Ty's ring around my finger. I still don't know why he gave it to me, but I'm glad. It's a grounding point for me, something to focus on to help control my anxiety. He notices me doing it and puts a hand on my knee. I jump but only because I didn't expect the touch. In all honesty, it feels pretty damn good.

"You're not a bad driver," I tell Ty as he follows the main

road into town. There isn't much need for directions, not in here, not in this little slice of Middle America. "I mean, for a guy who doesn't have a car." Ty smiles, but he doesn't respond, doesn't tell me how he learned to drive or when. I am laid out on the operating table for him to see, guts glistening shiny under fluorescent lights, while Ty is zipped up nice and tight, still this dark column of sin and mystery. I want to open him and look inside, see what makes him tick, what made him who he is, put all that hurt behind his eyes. I might be sorry when I do.

"So how do you know this guy's going to be at the Broken Glass?" Ty asks as he pulls into a parking space down the block from the building in question. I stare out the window and can't help but wonder how many of my sisters were conceived in the bathroom of this building or the alley behind it. I suspect at least two, creepy as that sounds. I open my door and put my heel on the step bar of the truck. The neon sign for the bar is glowing a bright, sickly green that seems at odds with the historical brick building it's housed in. India told me to look for a big, white truck with tinted windows and a mismatched camper shell. *Bingo.*

"Even if that wasn't his truck," I tell Ty with a raised eyebrow. "I would know he was here. I can practically smell him." Ty grabs my arm before I can jump out of the vehicle. His touch is gentle but firm. He wants to tell me something important.

"Revenge I can understand, but we also have to remember what the consequences of our actions could be. You and I, we've spent too long ignoring consequences. This is our chance at a fresh start, Nev, and much as I'd like to toss this piece of human garbage off a bridge, I don't want to spend the rest of my life pining for you from a jail cell." I smile back at Ty and lean back so that our faces are tantalizingly close.

"Guess what?" I whisper and Ty doesn't respond. He's too busy running his hand up my arm, brushing his fingers over the soft skin on my neck. "I haven't given a blow job in five years. I thought I'd ask if you'd let me practice on you." He laughs which wasn't my expected response and grabs me as I try to pull away.

"You have no idea how happy that makes me," he says as I roll my eyes. Ty tilts my head back and kisses me upside down, sloppy and sexy and absolutely, one hundred percent distracting. *I'm on a mission of revenge here, boy of my darkest dreams.*

"Wow, a guy excited over getting head? How rare is that?" Ty grabs me around the throat and licks his lips when I shiver. I let my head relax against his chest and don't even care that a bunch of people are stumbling out of the bar, laughing like a pack of diseased hyenas.

"I mean I'm happy that you haven't had your mouth wrapped around a bunch of other guys' dicks," Ty tells me, and it's my turn to laugh.

"You're a real piece of work," I say as I reach up and pull his hands away gently. "Now get off your ass and come help me beat the shit out of a man named Luis Clark." Ty laughs again and reluctantly lets me escape the cab of the truck. I might not be so lucky on the way home.

"Seriously?" he asks.

"As a heart attack." I hit the pavement in my heels, ducking into a slight crouch that actually makes me feel pretty fucking cool, like some kind of badass vampire chick or something. Maybe four inch pumps aren't your standard going-to-beat-the-shit-out-of-your-father's-murderer shoes, but I'll make do. Plus I have Ty, big, hard, thick, muscular Ty who punched the shit out of some convenience store robbers/wannabe rapists. What a memory. I spin Ty's ring around my finger while I wait for him to come around the front of the truck. Almost immediately he wraps his arm around my waist and pulls me against him.

"Noah made me kind of pissy, so forgive me if I'm feeling a bit possessive."

"I'm a woman," I tell Ty with a stare that says *Yeah, I like you where you are, but don't push it.* "Not a thing."

"And what a beautiful woman you are," Ty says and his bad boy charms work in disarming my feminist retort. Fine. He can put his arm around me. Whatever. My voting rights aren't at stake.

"So Noah … " Ty begins. "He's kind of a douche."

"Tyson McCabe," I say and he cringes. "Just shut up and help me find my revenge. I need it. It'll help fill up this gaping hole," I whisper as we pass by a group of stupid drunk country fucks. Ty stops me just outside the entrance to the bar and spins me to face him. He presses his ringed hand against the skin of my chest and closes his eyes. When he opens them, they're burning with dark fire, hot and sexy and absolutely deliciously deadly.

"Baby, I'll help you get your revenge, but trust me." Ty leans in and whispers in my ear, purposely nibbling on my chip earring with his teeth. "All you need to fill that hole is me." And then he pulls away abruptly and drags me into the dark smoky interior of the Broken Glass. I'm used to scenes like this; I've spent a very good portion of my young adult life in bars like this, but I'm not used to seeing the man of my nightmares bent over the bar with a drink in hand. My heart starts to bounce with anxiety and my lips go numb. I can't speak.

You wrapped your hands around his throat, and you didn't even care that I was watching, that you were burning me from the inside out, that with every breath my father never got to take, my heart was breaking in half, inch by inch. You ruined me; you ruined everything, and I want to fucking kill you.

I hold out my hand for a cigarette and find that Ty is already in the process of slipping one into my mouth. He lights us both up and then grabs my hand.

"Do you want to dance, Never?" he asks, giving me the most horrible case of déjà vu *ever.* I stare into Ty's eyes, and I can't move because I'm thinking all sorts of strange things like, *Thank God it's you and not Rick. I'm not into guys like Rick.* See, I was wrong before, oh so very wrong. I thought I needed someone to put me on the straight and narrow, but all I really needed was someone to take this crazy, fucked up ride with me, hug the curves of life's road and hold my hand the whole way. That's what I really needed. "This is your cue to say, *This is a bar, not a club,* and call me a whore," Ty whispers into my ear as he pulls me into his arms and guides me to an empty space between the old wooden tables. The fact that he remembers every detail of our first meeting is not lost on me. I smile at him and realize three things in that perfect second.

First, Ty is a perfectly nice guy. He might not be as nice a guy as Rick or Noah Scott, but that's okay because he's better that way, like coffee without cream, a bitter bite that hits all the right spots.

Second, he's the perfect fit to me, like that puzzle piece that was always missing, the one that got kicked under the couch and is only showing up now. It was meant to be there all along; I just hadn't found him yet.

The third thing is the most surprising. See, I had pegged Ty as a bad boy which, in effect, is true. He is *bad.* He's got piercings and tattoos and he cusses like a sailor and fucks like one, too, but he isn't a monster. Ty is the kind of guy you can take home to your family, show off, and know that at the end of the day, he'll be there for you. I'm now totally into guys like Ty. I shouldn't be, but I am. I think there's finally something going right with me. I don't *need* a guy like Ty to put me on the straight and narrow, to help me stop doing the things I shouldn't be doing and start doing the things I should, I just want him. By my side. *Forever.*

I close my eyes and let Ty swirl us around the dirty floor while the people around us drink and smoke and stare, wondering what these two crazy kids are doing slow dancing in the seediest bar in town. They can all go to hell as far as I'm concerned.

"Shame you don't dance anymore," Ty whispers as he pulls me close, sways us back and forth with the twangy country music that's playing too loudly in the background. "Because you're damn good at it."

"What would've happened if I had gone with you that night?" I whisper to Ty as he wraps his fingers in my hair and sighs against my skin. He can't get enough of me. He's always there touching, feeling, loving me. I have never had this before, not with anyone, not even with him. Noah Scott. "Would we have fucked and gone our separate ways?" I wonder aloud, not wanting to ruin the moment but needing to hear what he has to say about this. Don't ask why. It's just one of those things.

"I don't think so," Ty says back to me. "I mean, maybe we'd have fucked, but once I had you, I wouldn't have wanted to let you go."

"Liar."

"Nope, sorry, Nev." Ty stops dancing and grabs my face between his hands. I love it when he does that. His cigarette is hanging from his sexy lips, limp and crackling while his dark eyes burrow into me and his body reacts to mine. I can feel his erection through his pants, pressing into me, begging for another taste. "No lies, remember? I'm dead fucking serious here. I am like, head over friggin' heels, butterflies and puppies, hearts and fucking kitty cats in love with you." I try to turn away, but I'm smiling and shaking at the same time. It's just one of those things. "Seriously," Ty says as he turns me back towards him. "I am like a fucking Disney prince or some shit. Want me to sing for you? I could sing." I laugh and push away from him. This night is supposed to be about revenge, about showing Luis some pain, telling him how much he hurt me, hurt my sister, my family, and Ty has turned it into a date. "Let's just blow this fucking joint and forget about this sick son of a bitch," Ty says as he gestures at Luis' back.

"I want to," I begin, but I can't get out anymore words. I want to go with Ty, put this behind me, but until Luis knows that he hurt me, that he hurt my sister, I can't just walk away. I just *can't*. If I do, this demon could come back later, gnaw at my heart and break me. I have to deal with it now, while I have the chance. Ty looks at my face for a moment, nods and then moves past me. It takes me a second to realize what he's doing.

He steps up to Luis, a vision of art and color with his tattoos lit from within, fired up by the strange lighting above the bar, muscles tense, bracelets jingling. He taps the big, burly man on the shoulder and I have to hold back a rush of emotion as Luis turns and I get my first look at his face for a long, long while. *They chose him over me? How? Why?* I blink back my pity party. I have to because I'm the only one attending. If I don't leave now, I'll get stuck cleaning up the party and I've spent enough years doing just that.

Luis stares at Ty with his ugly, scruffy face. He has a wide, fat nose with mismatched nostrils and droopy eyelids, fat lips like a pair of earthworms, and a scowl that could curdle milk. My mother was normally a fan of handsome, younger men. Until she met Luis. Why him? I will never know. That is information I will never be privy to and for that, I'm grateful. I don't need to understand her.

"Are you Luis Clark?" Ty asks him, pleasant as could be. Luis sniffles and takes another sip of his beer.

"Who the fuck are you?" he asks him. Ty glances over at me as if to say, *He's all yours,* but I can't bring myself to move forward. If I do, I might kill him. I might rip Luis to shreds, tear him apart physically so he can see what I went through emotionally. I do not trust my own temper. Luis follows Ty's eyes and sees me. The air thickens and my cigarette drops from my lips, hits the floor and stays there. Nobody cares.

"Holy shit. Another Regali bitch," Luis says, standing up. "I can smell your kind from a mile away." I remember the *Fuck You* page from my now non-existent notebook. Just because I don't want to dwell on the past doesn't mean I can't learn from it.

"Fuck you," I say, and it feels so good that I find my chest expanding. Adrenaline pumps through my blood, swells my chests, makes my ears pound with the sound of a thousand drums. The music pauses briefly between songs and there's this bit of silence as the folks in the bar finally catch on that there's a problem. Misery loves company, of course, so they all turn and stare and hope that my life is worse than theirs. Thing is, it's not. Not anymore. "To the man that killed my father in cold blood." Luis stirs and starts to move forward. Ty grabs his fat, hairy arm with strong, sturdy fingers. "To the man that stole my life, who turned my family against me. To the man that tried to rape my sister, his own biological daughter, to you I say this." I take a deep breath, swallow my fear down and hope it helps staunch the bleeding of my soul. "You are the last person on earth I want to show mercy to, but the first person that has the pleasure of receiving it. You will not be the cause of my pain, not anymore, and you will not control me, directly or indirectly." I close my eyes and tilt my head back, just a bit, just enough that I feel this ... this *something* wash over and consume me. In a good way, of course. In a very, very good way.

"What the fuck are you babbling about?"

What Luis says makes no difference to me, no fucking difference. I drop my head and open my eyes.

"To you, the man whose life is darker even than my own, I say fuck you. Fuck you and go to hell." I grin and then realize that I've forgotten something. "Oh, yeah, and if you ever come near my family again, I will fucking chase you down and make you wish you were dead." Luis actually has the audacity to laugh at this and jerks his arm away from Ty's grasp.

"For that, you little cunt, you are next. I'm going to hold you down and – "

Ty steps in front of Luis, combat boots smashing into the floor with an almost audible sound. I swear, the wood nearly cracks with the heat of his passion. He looks at Luis for a moment and just when the big man is about to swing, Ty punches him straight in the face with his rings, sends him stumbling back where he smashes into the counter and collapses to a bleeding heap on the floor next to the bar stools. Nobody helps him up. Apparently, would-be rapists/murderers garner no sympathy here.

Ty removes his cigarette from his lips and blows out a puff of smoke.

"Don't talk to my girl like that, bitch," he says.

I leave that bar a new woman.

26

Time flies here. It's incredible. Days turn to weeks that are just one, endless span of life, all of this fighting and making up, these moments of just remembering to breathe. There are sweet, sharp moments with Noah (who I haven't let go of yet but who I owe so much to) and my family, hot, dark ones with Ty, and a whole lot of hurting and healing. The process, I have come to understand, is not one that can have a beginning and an end. It's something that's continuous, forever being expanded upon. I can't just have this epiphany where I'm all better again. That will never happen. What I can do is make sure that each day is better than the last, and if it's not, I have to figure out why, understand it, break it down. Ty makes that so easy for me. He's the only thing that's remaining constant right now, holding me in place while everything else spins around me. He tucks my head under his chin at night, holds me and whispers sweet words (or dirty ones) until I fall asleep. I feel more rested than I have in years. No more crying at night, not for me.

"You do know that it's totally lame to put up a tree like four days before Christmas?" I tell Beth as we scramble to get the lights on, so the little girls can start hanging ornaments. Zella, whose phone calls I've been avoiding like the plague, says that if the decorations aren't up by the time she gets here then she's going to turn around and head straight back to Texas. I want to talk to her, I really do, but I want to wait until I can see her face. More than ever I believe that most of communication takes place through body language, and I'm afraid that if Zella and I can't look into one another's eyes, that something might get lost in translation.

"I didn't see you doing anything about it before now," Beth says around a light bulb. She's stuck it between her teeth and is trying to wrestle a broken one out of the strand. The strand is winning.

"Well," I say as I glance over at Ty who's sitting cross legged on the sofa, untangling yet another strand of old, white lights. "I didn't have the time for it." Ty senses that I'm talking about him and looks up, meeting my eyes with a flash of sin that tells me I'm in trouble later. I make myself a note to stop by the store today and get more condoms. We've gone through a whole box and then some. Maybe it's because we're both still sex addicts, will always be sex addicts. Or maybe it's just because he's so fucking hot. Hard to say.

I step back and examine the tree with a sick feeling in my gut. I'm standing in the living room, yes, the living room, after all this time. The memories of my father's death aren't gone, not by a long shot, but since Ty and I confronted Luis, I'm not so afraid of them anymore. I can look at them without breaking down, without running into the arms of a stranger. After all, if I need to run into anybody's arms, I can run into Ty's. And now finally, I can truly, honestly say that I'm not mad at my dad, not anymore. He didn't choose to die. He didn't choose to leave me with that woman who even now is looking into the living room with a sour expression on her face and sea turtle earrings hanging from her stretched out earlobes. And as far as not being around when he was alive, I can't blame him. My mother makes even the best of occasions uncomfortable.

"That's organically grown?" she asks which is such a stupid fucking question that nobody answers her. Nobody except Noah Scott. He steps into the living room in his coat and gloves and sets the last box of decorations down on the floor. They've been kept in the barn for years and are not in the best of shape, but we've decided to go through them all, make a proper Christmas for the little ones. It makes all the sense in the world to me. I have to give something back to them. These past few weeks have been ... interesting. I've gotten to know the ones I left and the ones I never knew, but it hasn't been easy, and we're just getting started. Plus, Zella gets back today and who the hell knows how that might go.

"Of course, Ms. Regali," Noah says with a smile, and I notice that my mother gives him a lingering look that makes my stomach sick. She might think shes some free spirited, hippie who's changing the world with her cage free eggs and the vegetarian meatloaves she makes for her new boyfriend, but she's not fooling anyone. She is a selfish caricature of a person, and I have taken to simply ignoring her.

"Yeah, Mom," I say and I try to make my smile look real pretty when I continue. Maybe she won't know I'm being sarcastic. "Because in the Midwest, we always make sure to import organic Christmas trees. It's a big issue 'round here." My mother stares at me but says nothing. It's Beth who takes the reigns. She's my soul momma.

"Never, grab me that next strand if you would." I roll my eyes as my mom leaves for yet another date and lean down to grab the lights. Noah and I end up brushing hands as we both go for it and get caught staring at one another. It's so hard to look at him everyday and know he can't be mine. He just can't be. If I could have him *and* Ty ... well, I don't know what I'd do, but I can't, and there is no way in hell that I can lose McCabe. It just isn't happening. I could list you reasons, but then you'd never escape. My love for him is endless. And when we're together, just me and him, I can't even think about Noah Scott, but then, I can't find anything wrong with Noah either, anything to discredit him. I was in love with him, never stopped being in love with him, but maybe I need to take a step back and look at this from a different point of view. Ty McCabe is Never Ross' soul mate; Never Regali belonged to Noah Scott. She is long dead, so I think it's time I said something to Noah before he gets hurt, really hurt. I can't do that to him again. He's been waiting around for me all this time. At the very least, I owe him a hug and an apology. We could be good friends, I think, if he lets us be. He may not. Right now though is not the time. I don't know when or if there'll be a perfect moment, but I can't say anything with my sisters and Ty around. Things wouldn't be so awkward if they didn't keep inviting him over. He even stops by on his own half the time, catches up with us when we're on walks, sits next to us while we read. I know he loves me, but I just can't love him back, not more than I love Ty.

"I hope Zella appreciates all this work," I say instead as I flop down next to Ty. My stomach is roiling and making me nauseous. I blame India's cooking. Last night, she wanted to make me something special and tried to whip up some homemade mac 'n' cheese. It tasted like dog shit, but I ate it anyway. For her. Always for her. I think, also, that I'm feeling ill because of Zella's homecoming. She was not so supportive when I left, and she seems the least shook up that I was even gone. Maybe she doesn't even care? I swallow hard and spin Ty's ring around my finger. Since he gave it to me, I haven't taken it off, not even once.

"I hope so," Ty says as he stands up and passes Beth the strand he was working on. "Because she's damn lucky to have a family like yours. The closest thing I ever had to a brother was my cousin, and he died a long time ago." I pause; Noah pauses; Beth pauses. Even Lettie who's coming in to hand me a cup of sweet tea pauses. They may not know exactly how rare it is to hear Ty talk about his past, but they can sense it. This is big. Ty is revealing a piece of himself to us. I don't know why he's chosen this moment, but the words just seem to slip past his sexy lips and sit heavy with us in our room of lights and wreaths and plastic, chubby, fat fucking Santa Claus's. "My mother ran him over with her SUV," Ty says and we all just sort of sit there in stunned silence.

"Um, here," Lettie says, realizing even at thirteen that maybe she better go, that maybe this isn't a conversation for her to join in on. Even Beth seems uncomfortable. Noah, though, oh, I don't know about him. He just seems sad for Ty. He's sort of selfless like that.

"I'm so sorry," he tells Ty, and it's weird to see Ty look up at him with a sad smile. Ty and Noah might not be friends, but in the last two weeks, they've gotten used to one another. I hope that one day, we could all be dead honest with each other and just be friends. I would like that. A lot. The first boy I loved and the last boy I will ever love.

"He was six," Ty says randomly and then, "Anybody up for a cigarette?" He stands up quickly and moves out the front door. I follow close behind him and we sit together on the porch swing.

"Want to talk about it?" I say, wondering how the hell anybody could run over a kid with an SUV. His mother must've been either very self absorbed or very drunk. Despite the photos of cars Ty has in his apartment and the beautiful rings, I decide then and there that I'm probably going to hate his mother as much as I hate mine.

"Nope," he says as he passes me a cig and we smoke in silence. Snow is starting to fall ever so gently from the sky, drifting down to the ground in powdery flakes that melt on contact, leaving the dirt driveway a mess of mud and slush. Neither of us is wearing shoes, and it's awfully cold outside, so Ty and I snuggle up and watch tendrils of smoke curl in the chilly air. "This is too fucking perfect to ruin." I sigh and close my eyes, letting Ty hold me in an armful of butterflies. I've counted them all – there are thirty in total – and I'm working on memorizing each species, each color, each size. They're like freckles or something, just this other, different, unique bit of Ty McCabe that I have to know.

"When?" I ask him. "When are you gonna tell me?"

"Soon," Ty promises, and I believe him because he hasn't given me reason to think otherwise. "When I'm ready, baby, you can cut me open and dig through what's left." I almost tell him there's no need, that all I really need from him is his heart and that, I'm pretty sure, I already have.

27

So India goes to the store to pick up some stuff for this horribly ostentatious dinner that Beth is going to cook in honor of our family being whole once again while I sit in nervous anticipation at the bottom of the staircase, an unlit cigarette hanging out of my mouth, and a lump in my stomach. Things are going so well that I can't help but worry that Zella will change everything.

"She's really excited to see you, you know," Noah tells me

as he finally finds a moment of peace away from my sisters and takes off his winter coat, hanging it on a hook in the hallway. Beth has the heater up way too high, even for this weather, and Noah and I both have little beads of sweat on our foreheads. He sits down next to me and touches his fingers to the back of my hand. I should probably pull away, but I don't because I'm a coward. I never was before, but with Noah, I suddenly feel that way. It's not a good place to be.

"How do you know?" I ask him and then hold up a finger to stop him from answering. "No, wait. Let me guess. You guys are pen pals or something equally as disturbing." Noah blinks his big blue eyes at me for a moment and finally laughs like he's just got the joke.

"Actually, sort of," he says as he adjusts his sky blue T-shirt. It's got these words in Latin scribbled across it that I can barely read. *Amicitiae nostrae memoriam spero sempiternam fore.* I think I know what it means, but I don't mention it because I'm afraid I might be wrong. *I hope that the memory of our friendship will be everlasting.* I pray to some blind eyed, shadow faced deity that Noah really believes that. I'd love to have him as a friend. "We e-mail sometimes." He shrugs like it's not that big of a deal although I know it is. I can still read him. Noah Scott is like an open book. He isn't like Ty at all; Noah lets his emotions play across his face like a movie.

"You know," I say as I put my hand over the top of his and squeeze it, more friendly than anything else. "I never did thank you." He looks me and then runs his other hand through his blonde hair.

"For what?"

"For waiting around for me," I tell him and before he can protest, I throw him a piece of his own poetry, give him something to think about. Or at least to dissuade him from trying to protest. We both know the truth, so there's no point in pretending otherwise. Besides, Ty is no poet. Noah is still my favorite manipulator of the English language. I pull my cigarette from my lips and hold it between my fingers. "*Buried by blood,*" I began and Noah groans, pulling his hand away and putting it over his face. Normally he doesn't mind his stuff being thrown around, not even when it's bad, but this, this is the last poem in the Butterfly Series, and I think he's actually embarrassed to hear it aloud. It is sort of personal. "*Gasping; As if air could be bought with wishes and prayers.*" I smile as Noah sighs and surprisingly, picks up the passage.

"*I am drowning; Here it is, my final plea.*" I chuckle and try to keep my voice steady as I continue. This poem, when I first read it, sent me spiraling into depression for days. Now, though, it doesn't seem so bad anymore. It gives Noah depth. Maybe, one day, he'll fall in love with another girl and she'll see that just as Ty sees my bad memories and my pain and my fear and loves that, too.

"*Just remember, I won't repeat, so pay attention; Write it down.*"

"*I am bleeding and in my own blood, I am drowning.*"

"*I didn't know how hard it would hit me when my lungs breathed it in.*"

"*I didn't know how sad I would feel as I watched my own vision, dimming.*"

"*I didn't realize how much I would miss you in that last moment and how much I would cry.*" We look at each other just as Ty appears at the top of the stairs. I hope he's not intimidated, but no, not Ty McCabe. Not by a long shot.

"*I cried and the tears mixed with the blood and I couldn't see them because red filled my vision and then I was blind and then I cried no more and then the bleeding stopped; It stopped when my heart stopped; My heart; The one that was broken by you, could only have been broken by you, and I was happy because I could never bleed again."*

Noah and I both spin around as Ty recites the final stanza of the poem without a hitch, without a single misplaced word. He must've found it in my suitcase and read it. That would be oh so typical Ty. I hope he doesn't mind that I brought them here with me. It just seemed appropriate.

"That's one sick ass piece of poetry," Ty tells Noah and then he just turns around and walks away, disappearing into my bedroom to, hopefully, put on some kind of shirt. If he keeps walking around without one, one of my sisters may very well try and jump him. Or maybe I'm just projecting because that's what I want to do.

I look at Noah quickly, expecting him to be angry or sad or upset, but he's just smiling away like all is right with the world. He's too happy like that, Noah is.

"I like him," he tells me with a smile that says he suspects how much Ty means to me. At first I think he's admitting defeat, getting ready to do the hard thing and announce to both us that this will never work. "Too bad I'm going to have to kick his ass." And then Noah leans over and presses the softest, lightest kiss to my lips before standing up and moving into the kitchen to help Beth. *Crap.* My stomach rolls over and I barely make it to the bathroom before I throw up. As soon as I'm done, I go outside and smoke like a chimney while I try to figure out what I'm going to do.

"Any sparkles or butterflies?" Ty asks, coming out the door in a tight as fuck red tee and baggy ass holey jeans tucked into his big, brown boots. His shirt says, *Can't Be Bothered,* but his dark hair is gelled and styled to perfection and his facial piercings are different, all small, silver studs, even his nose ring which has been replaced with a small bar. His rings are all silver now, too, without any gems other than the beautiful blue one I was admiring on the bus. "Any fireworks or explosions of light and sound?" Ty makes this stupid hand motion that reminds me of jazz hands. Ugh.

"He kissed me," I respond automatically and Ty shrugs. He pauses at the edge of the porch and slides my cigarette out of my mouth, sticking it in between his own lips with a grin.

"And I sucked you off last night so screw him."

"Ty, Jesus Christ!" I say, but I'm glad he's not mad.

"You ready to say it yet?" he asks me as a car turns down the driveway and my blood goes cold in my veins. Bitch-Never starts freaking out and comes running around the back of the barn at full speed like she's a guard dog or something. Could be one if she wanted. Noah was right: she bites. I have the marks to prove it.

"Say what?" I whisper, but I'm too distracted by my sister's car to say or do much of anything. The white sedan winds its way towards us slowly, crawling towards a conclusion, holding the last living member of my family that I need to make up with to move forward with my life. This has been a slow journey but a worthwhile one.

"Fuck Noah Scott," Ty whispers into my ear. "Say it now or I'll make you scream it tonight." I punch him in the arm as Zella comes to a stop awfully close to the porch steps. I want to indulge him but I can't, not right now. I need my mind wholly and completely focused on Ty McCabe when I say it. Luckily, he's not as easily offended as some. He gets me, as always.

I start to step forward and find that I'm down the porch stairs before I even realize that I've moved. Snow is still falling lightly from the gray sky, resting on my scalp like a halo or something. I brush flakes from my eyelashes as Zella climbs out of the car with a head of dyed brunette curls and a face that's red and soaked in tears. I don't, of course, know why she's crying, but some part of me hopes it's because she's happy to see me.

For once, I'm right.

"Never," she says and then she's running and we're throwing ourselves in one another's arms. She squeezes the life out of me and whispers in my ear, "You were right." And that is all I need to hear. I don't know how she knows I needed that or if Beth told her or what, and I don't give a shit. All I want to do right now is hold my sister tight and know that things will be okay. I was afraid of seeing her, but only because I didn't want to lose the progress I'd already made. Looks like I didn't need to be. Things are looking up. They might not be for long, but they are right here, right now, and I'm starting to understand that that's all I can ever ask for. "Oh my God, Never," Zella says as she steps back and looks down.

I'm not wearing shoes and my feet are freezing in the icy slush of the driveway, but I don't care. The relief I'm starting to feel spread through my chest is enough to keep me warm. For now.

"Let's go inside," she says with a shiver, catching Ty with her eye as she passes. She tosses me a, *You will tell me about this man or you will die,* look and drags me inside. When she sees Noah, she squeals and the two of them hug tight, like the oldest of friends. "It's like the good ol' days," she says to me as she looks at Noah and I standing next to each other. "I always thought you guys made the cutest couple."

Ah. Noah and I exchange a look and then I exchange one with Ty who just smiles. He isn't worried. Things get awkward for a second, but luckily I find that I'm easily able to distract Zella by discussing her hair which she says is the worst dye job she's ever gotten, but seems quite proud of.

"I don't see why you two had to dye your hair," Beth tells us as she motions for us all to cluster into the teeny little kitchen that was never meant for a gathering such as this, but which accommodates us all without complaint. Things are tight but cozy. It's a strange feeling but a pleasant one.

The four little girls get chairs and the rest of us stand. People are talking all around me, gesturing, firing off questions that hit the tip of their tongues and disappear into this mass of bodies and voices and feelings that swirl like leaves in the wind and just when I think it's all too overwhelming to take in, too much to absorb all at once, Ty is there and squeezing my hand with his. My anxiety dissipates in a blip and is gone in a flash, giving me a chance to look at Zella who's planning on becoming the 'world's best damn defense lawyer' and Beth who is such a mom now that it's almost comical; there's Jade who's sad but not lost, India who sings like a siren, and Lettie who sketches when she thinks nobody is looking. There's Lorri, the little girl with big dreams of Broadway, and Darla who will know me throughout her life without a single gap, who will be Maple's big sister instead of her aunt. And then there's me, Never Nicholas Ross who was once Never Fontaine Regali, who doesn't know what she wants to do, but who's in love with a guy named Tyson McCabe that has a past he won't speak of and hands that can play my body like an instrument.

Things are good. Almost, dare I say, perfect. I even smile when Beth hands me a bowl of hot, peeled potatoes and says, "Mash."

"I hate mashed potatoes," I tell her, but I do it anyway, if only because it feels good to participate in this group mentality we have going on. Zella smiles at me from across the kitchen and I know that as soon as we get time alone, I'm going to tell her my story, my whole story. I don't know why, but something about her makes me want to spill my secrets. She's going to be a damn good lawyer.

"Never and I are guests, we shouldn't have to prepare anything. We should be catching up on the couch with a couple of beers."

"Not at nineteen you're not," Beth says with a tight-lipped smile. "Not on my watch."

"Alcohol Nazi," Zella says affectionately. "You do know that I drink at school, right?"

"Sorry, Zella," Beth says as she sets a plate of overcooked pasta on the table. "That's just the way it's going to be. Period." I laugh, they all do, but then I get caught on a word, the one that means end of sentence and woman's menstrual cycle in three tiny syllables.

Period. Wait. Shit.

28

It is so official. I am fucked. I am up shit creek without a paddle. I am batshit friggin' crazy.

Ty and I arrived here on the seventh of December. It's now the twenty-first. We made love on the fourth. I always, *always,* get my period on the fifteenth. Well, where the fuck is it? I go on my phone under the table during dinner even though I get bitched at by Beth. I end up having to freaking ask Lacey to research it for me and get back to me. Maybe my period is just late? It's never been before, but it is now. It is fucking now. I text Lacey with a few, minor details and don't even bother to try and hide the fact that I'm worried. She sends me some stupid emoticon faces and says she'll call me later.

"You look like you've seen a ghost," Ty tells me at one point, but I can't even look at his face. We had sex, a lot of sex, without condoms, and I'm seriously surprised by this? Wow. Good job, Never. Way to go on taking control of your sex life. I try to smile and laugh at my sisters' jokes, try to tell Zella something interesting about my life, but all I can think about is this.

I might be pregnant.

I try to tell myself that *might* is a very important word and that I can't worry about it yet. Then I start thinking about what I would do if I was pregnant and things don't seem so rosy anymore. Abortion? Adoption? Single parent? Family? Which option will I get? Some of them are choices; others are not. If I am pregnant and Ty finds out, he could take off. He doesn't look like the daddy type with his rings and his piercings and his *fuck this and fuck that* attitude.

"I don't think the Sharks have a chance," Noah says in reference to hockey or basketball or some other stupid sport that I don't give a rat's ass about.

"Fuck the Sharks," Ty says, and somehow that comment just makes me sick to my stomach. Or maybe it's just Beth's nasty wheat rolls. Or the baby. Or yeah, it could be that. I run to the bathroom and throw up, surprised as fuck to find that Ty has picked the door's lock and come in behind me. He holds my hair back and tries to be soothing. "Your sister is *the* world's worst cook," he says. "I thought India was bad, but wow, Beth takes the cake."

I don't answer him. Presently, I'm neck deep in toilet water and puke, so it's sort of not an option. I'm also afraid that I can't look at him without blurting it out. There's also the possibility that he'll see it in my eyes. Ty seems to be able to read me like a freaking book.

"Go away," I moan, but he just sits on the counter and waits for me. Afterward, we pop out front for a cigarette. I vaguely realize that if I am pregnant, that smoking might not be the best thing in the world for me, but I do it anyway because otherwise, I don't know what I'll do. Run through the house screaming is more like it. Maybe I should fuck, Ty, you know? Might as well, right? Can't hurt.

"Are you feeling any better?" Noah asks, coming out the door with a cup of clear soda in one hand and a straw in the other. He tries to pass these to me, and I stare at him like he's a crazy person. If I was pregnant with his baby, things might be different. Noah has money and family ties and he's the perfect sort of dude for something as strange and foreign as fatherhood. I glance at Ty and watch him blow puffs of smoke into the air. *Shit.*

"Thanks," I say, but I don't take the items. I still feel like shit. Can morning sickness hit this quick? I pull out my phone and text Lacy again. There's already a poorly written text waiting for me.

K nev internet says stress could cause late perid. I stare at her misspelled word and suddenly want to choke the life out of someone. Could be her, could be someone else. Preferably, it's me. I'm the dumb ass here. Me *and* Ty.

And? I type. *Anything else?*

Could also be preggers tho. Wow. How helpful is that? *so glad to be a dyke 2day.*

More info would be nice, Lacey. I am freaking the fuck out over here, and I can't get online without getting nagged and bombarded. Hurry, please.

"Girl talk?" Ty asks with his head tilted to the side. "Or can I be creepy and read it all?" I roll my eyes and ignore him. Noah, in an effort not to look awkward with the soda and straw, sticks the striped thing in the cup and drinks it.

morning scknss can strt as early as 2 wks but usually not. go get a test frm the stre. luv u grl and cant wait to c u. miss you.

I sigh and turn off my phone. She's kind of sweet but also kind of dumb. I slip my phone back in my pocket and start a fresh cig. I'm going to need a whole truckload of them to survive until I find out.

"Never," Lorri says, opening the door and gesturing wildly. "Come back inside. We're playing charades!"

"The game of champions," Ty says as Noah touches my arm lightly on his way inside. I try to follow, but Ty stops me. "Everything okay?" he asks, and there's this moment that changes everything because despite my better judgment, I lie.

"Yep, everything's fine."

Then I spend the rest of the evening wallowing in how I've practically ruined everything that Ty and I have built together by not telling the truth. I try to explain to myself that I don't know for sure yet, but that as soon as I do, I will tell him. It doesn't make things any easier. Fortunately, with the help of a very small glass of wine, I manage to make it through the evening which, actually, is pretty amazing. I have friends and family and everything is so fucking festive and joyous that it sort of knocks me back a bit. It's been *years* since I've been a part of anything like this. And even longer since I was able to whoop Noah's ass at Twister.

Ty stays a bit more quiet than usual, watches me a bit more carefully, which in turn makes me want to avoid him. By the time everyone else is in bed and he and I are standing together in my room, he's ready to get all pissy about it.

"Are you avoiding me?" he asks which sucks because I was.

"Kind of," I admit, refusing to poison the air between us with any more lies. Ty pulls off his shirt and throws it over the back of my chair. He's been so cool this whole time and now he's getting pissed. Not good. Not now.

"Why?" he asks me as I strip down to my bra and underwear. The fact that I'm getting naked isn't lost on him. "And don't try to distract me with sex," he says as I drop to my knees and reach for the buttons on his jeans. When I glance up at him, he licks his lips and takes a massive breath.

"Why not?" I ask, all innocent like. I'm not trying to be deceitful or to hurt him, but I need more time and besides, even after all this time, I have yet to fulfill my promise of a blow job. Ty and I just can't seem to last with any other activity than full throttle fucking.

"You are such a tease," he says as he wraps his ringed fingers in my hair and opens his pants with his other hand. "How am I supposed to say no to that?"

29

I wake up in the middle of the night in a cold sweat.

Ty is sleeping peacefully next to me, face blissful and quiet. I stare at him for a long, long time and try to figure out if I should wake him up and tell him. I could ask him to take me to the store and we could do this together, find out together. I trace his nose with my finger, brush my hand across his gently parted lips. He moans, but he doesn't stir.

He lays still, wrapped in my yellow sheets with one hand curled above his head and the other resting on his belly just above his cock. His eyelashes lay across his cheeks, dark and perfect, and the sculpted perfection of his cheeks is even more beautiful than I thought possible, bathed in moonlight and the soft kiss of night.

I lean over and whisper words across his mouth, soft breathy words that I know he can't hear, but that I have to say.

"Forgive me, I lied to you." I kiss his mouth lightly, so lightly that my presence is as noticeable as a butterfly, soft and gentle. "I want to tell you, but I have to know first. Once I do, no matter what, I'll say it. I will. I know I will." I rub my thumb across one of Ty's eyebrows, the one with the ring in it, and smile down at him, praying that he doesn't wake up and find me missing.

When I stand up, I feel dizzy and lightheaded. I can't say if it really is because I'm pregnant or because I'm just nervous, but it isn't pleasant. I'm planning on going to Beth's room when I notice that there are lights on downstairs. I have to see who it is and what they're doing before I make any decisions. I don't want anyone else to know except her, except for the woman who's my mom but isn't.

Luckily, that's exactly who I find.

"Beth," I say, feeling so small and miserable and helpless. I have fucked up again. I have fucked everything up. I sort of want to die in that moment. After all that's happened, I couldn't learn, couldn't do one, tiny little thing differently. My sister is reading a book on the couch, in the living room where we both lost the man who was our daddy. I see my father's face floating above the coffee table and have to close my eyes so tight they hurt. I hear the couch creak and soon Beth is up and by my side, taking me into her arms and holding me tightly.

"What's wrong, honey?" she asks, and I can't say what I have to say because it is so friggin' stupid. Beth strokes my hair back and sways back and forth with me in time to the wind outside the windows. It's comforting enough that after a few swallows, I can actually speak the words I hate to speak. As if I wasn't cliched enough, as if playing the drinking-smoking-fucking bad girl wasn't enough, I had to go ahead and layer on this, too.

"I think I might be pregnant," I say and start to sob. After all this time, all these fucks, this particular problem has never happened to me, not ever. And now it has. With Ty, the one person in the world that it should happen with. Just not yet. Not now. "Help me."

"Oh, Never," Beth says, but she doesn't sound disappointed which is nice. I had sort of thought she would be. Then again, she's twenty-three with a two year old, so she really has no room to judge. "You sound just like me when I found out. Ty?"

"Of course," I say because thankfully, it can only be his. There's no other possibility unless we're looking at the immaculate conception here. *Thank God I haven't slept around lately.* I imagine how I would've handled this back at the dorms, before I met Ty, when I didn't know the names of the men I was sleeping with. It might've killed me. "But I haven't told him because I might be wrong, so … " Beth nods her head and kisses me on the forehead. I dash away my tears and vow that those are all I get. I made my bed and now I'll sleep in it. Besides, I am sick and fucking tired of crying.

"Grab your coat," she says and then drives us to the store where we stock up on four different brands of tests, all of them in pretty, flowery packages that don't even begin to describe how I feel about this. I wish there was a black and red box, one that said *Are you knocked up?* on the side because that's the one I would get. It would be even better if the little plus sign was a middle finger. That, at least, would be somewhat funny. Nothing is funny right now.

The clerk rings up the four boxes with raised eyebrows which makes me absolutely, one hundred percent livid.

"You have a problem, you country bumpkin piece of shit?" I ask and have to leave the store to keep control of my temper. It's been quiet lately, much quieter than usual, and now this whole thing has revived it to angry dragon status. At least I don't feel the urge to go out and drown my pain. That feeling is almost completely gone now, and I don't think it had anything to do with SOG or my celibacy and that it has everything to do with Ty McCabe.

Beth and I drive home in silence. I think she knows that I don't want to discuss anything with anyone right now.

"If you need to talk," she says when we pull up in front of the house, but I don't, so I remain quiet and retreat into the downstairs bathroom to piss on some plastic sticks.

Only when the double bars and the little plus signs come up on all eleven tests do I know how much trouble I'm really in.

30

I can't look at Ty the next morning. I know he knows that something is wrong, but I just can't tell him what that thing is. It's horrible, so horrible. I have a feeling that he's going to freak the fuck out when he finds out. What if he just runs away and leaves me like this? What am I going to do without him? Still, I promised I would tell him, so that's what I'm going to do. I'm going to clear the air between us and go back to being honest. He got one fuck up, so I should get one, too.

"Ty?" I ask as I come up behind him in the kitchen and see that he's in the process of making us some toast. It's always us. He never just makes food for himself. Even though he can barely boil an egg, I appreciate that from the bottom of my heart. It's just one of those gestures that you can never get enough of.

"Yeah?" he asks as I come in and sit down at the table behind him. My heart is racing like a herd of elephants, drowning out any logical or reasonable thoughts. I'm in a suspended state of panic right now, stuck somewhere between knowing what I'm going to do and having no fucking clue. I'm a twenty-one year old, unmarried college student with a poor family and a boyfriend who's just quit his job and is getting ready to move into the dorms.

Fuck.

"I was wondering if you'd like to walk to the park with me today." We've walked there several times before. It's just down the road and although it isn't anything special, this park is nearly always empty in winter giving it this sort of private feel that I like. When I'm there, it feels like nothing in the world can interfere, like I'm standing in my own little bubble with only the people I've brought along with me. Ty, of course, has gone on every walk, so I figure he'll go on this one just the same, not knowing that I'm going to drop a friggin' bomb on his head when we get there. Unfortunately, something in my voice must have tipped him off because he puts his hands on the counter and closes his eyes.

"This has to do with you avoiding me last night, doesn't it?" *No lies, Never.*

"Yes."

"And the fact that you disappeared on me last night?" My blood goes cold. He knows I left? Shit, damn, and fuck me. What does he think? What does he suspect?

"Yes."

Ty breathes out and doesn't breathe back in for the longest time, so long that I'm suddenly afraid he's dead and gone. It makes my stomach ache and my heart break in two. Of course, that's just me overreacting to this horrible, cold lump of fear I have in my belly that says Ty is going to run out on me, leave me alone with this partially healed heart and this decision that hangs over my head like my own, personal rain cloud.

"Let's go," he says, grabbing the pieces of bread from the toaster and handing one over to me. "Let's go and you can tell me whatever it is that you need to tell me, but God, Never, if you break my heart I don't know how I'm going to survive."

31

Ty and I bundle up in scarves and coats and boots. I wear a miniskirt which he raises his eyebrows at because although it may not be snowing, it's still cold as fuck outside. I put on knee high socks and wear it anyway. Neither of us wears gloves.

We manage to escape the house with India's help although I do feel guilty about leaving my little siblings behind. We've had a few amazing days at the park, days that rank right up there with some of the best in my life. We took Darla and Maple down slides, watched a family of birds in the trees and played chase with bitch-Never. Now though, it's just me and Ty. Alone. He takes my hand in his as soon as we hit the porch and pulls out a cigarette from his pocket with the other. When he hands it to me, I stick it in the pocket of my own coat. My mouth waters and my hands feel shaky, but I know I can't smoke. Not anymore. I try to console my addiction by promising it that this is oh so temporary and that I'll be back to smoking in no time. *Yeah, nine fucking months,* it complains, and I soon find myself leaning over next to Ty so I can catch the hint of tobacco in the air, draw it into my lungs and bathe in it. Pathetic. I'm as addicted to cigarettes as I was to sex.

"Want to tell me what this is about?" Ty asks as we walk down the driveway and pause at the main road. No cars. Typical. It's always been quiet out here. I hope that one day, when my mother is gone, that I can live here again, make the house my own. Beth would probably snatch it up first, but you never know. Besides, I'd have to be able to travel if I did that, be able to leave at the drop of a hat because I don't think I could be stuck in a town like this forever. As a place to hang my hat it might be okay, especially if I was between trips to Japan, India, France, Germany, wherever.

"Not yet," I tell him, and I know how bad that sounds, but I want to be sitting down, want both of us sitting down. It could be a bench, a swing set, a slide, I don't care as long as we've got our butts on something for support. After all, this is the kind of news that rocks your world. Best to take it with the ground a few inches closer to your head, just in case you pass out.

I sigh.

"Don't freak, okay?" I say which probably makes things worse. Ty bites at his lip.

"Is this about me?" he asks, and I give him a look. He raises his eyebrows at me and shrugs. "Sorry, but I don't see why you can't just tell me. I mean, it must be pretty fucking terrible if you can't just spit it out."

"Ty, stop," I say, but he's already gone silent, fallen into this thoughtful darkness that is as attractive as it is scary. I wonder briefly what he was like as a whore. Did he talk to his clients? Did he even know their names? Did they cuddle afterward? I shiver. One day, I will have to know the answers to these questions. As of right now, I'm content with pushing them back. One thing at a time, please. "It's not the worst thing in the world," I say honestly, knowing that to me, the worst things in the world are molestation, rape, torture, and murder. I mean, compared to those things, this is cake, this is easy.

Yeah, right.

"Is this about Noah?" Ty asks, freezing like a deer in the headlights. I roll my eyes and grab his arm. My fingers tingle when they touch him, even through the fabric of his coat.

"Come on."

Ty follows me down a short trail that cuts straight across a field and into the park. There's a road to get here by car but folks rarely use it. The trail is deep and cuts through the dry grass like a wound. This is the kind of park that everyone walks to.

The sky is about as gray as it can get, solid, uninterrupted. No sunshine peaks through and no clouds float by, but something about it is a bit mystical, like it's this otherworldly vortex, something that could suck me up and take me away. I look over at Ty, at his pinched lips and his worried eyes, and I know that I don't want to be sucked up or taken away; I want to be right here, with him, even if it's hard. That's what makes it worth it. I take a deep breath. I can do this.

"Swing with me?" I ask him as I watch his eyes sweep across the bare limbs of trees, follow a flock of dark birds into the sky, and come to rest on the playground to our right. It's a big, plastic colorful thing with two slides, one yellow and one purple, and a green tunnel with small, grimy windows that Darla and Maple refused to leave for the longest time. They just sat in there and stared at us while we waved and encouraged them to come out. Finally Beth had to go up and get them. Strange kids, my relations.

"Let's go up there," Ty says as he points at the platforms above us. There's a ladder leading up to them along with a small rock wall. Ty pulls his hand away from me and has halfway scaled the damn wall before I even get over there. I watch his ass as he tries to wedge his big boots onto the fake, rubber rocks and try not to laugh.

"You're certainly something, aren't you?" I joke as I take the easy way up and crawl into the tunnel on my belly. Ty gets stuck about three quarters of the way up and has to do a bizarre little jig to get his foot on the platform and join me. When he does, he's panting for breath. "Out of shape much?" I ask him jokingly and he grins.

"Guess so," he says as he squats in front of me and reaches for my hands, pulling me out of the tunnel and into his lap. "I haven't worked out in weeks. I think I'm getting a beer belly." I reach my fingers under Ty's coat and shirt and feel the hard planes of his abs. No way in hell. I shake my head.

"Not even close," I tell him and he smiles, but there are no dimples there. He might be joking around with me, but he's worried, terrified maybe. I can only guess what he's thinking, but if his mind is on Noah Scott, nothing good will come of it. I take a deep breath and open my mouth to say it, to just blurt it out for all the world to hear.

I'm pregnant, Ty. I'm pregnant with your baby, and I don't know what to do. We're finally getting our lives together and now this happens. Will you help me? Can you help me? I love you, but I'm not sure I can handle this. I put my hand on my belly and part my lips.

"Wait," Ty says as he grabs me by my upper arms and flips me over, lightning quick, pressing my back into the rubber platform of the play structure. It happens so fast that I nearly get the breath knocked out of me. He holds my wrists down on either side of my head and just stares at me like even he doesn't know what he's doing.

"Before you say whatever it is that you're going to say, can I show you something?" he asks as the fog of his breath tangles and dances with mine in the crisp winter air.

"Ty, you don't – "

He cuts me off.

"Please." He says the word like it's a question, but it's not. He's not asking my permission. Ty is telling me that he's going to show me whether I like it or not, so I better be ready for it. "I need to show you how much you rock my fucking world." And then Ty is kissing me hot and hungry, down my neck and back up again. He's biting my lip and making me bleed, brushing his lips across the beating pulse in my neck, the one that throbs like crazy when he's around.

"Ty, stop," I say because we're on a playground for God's sake, but he doesn't. He doesn't stop. He adjusts my wrists so that he's holding them with one hand, and although I probably could fight him if I wanted to, I don't. I don't want him to stop, not now, not ever.

Ty reaches under my shirt and coat and somehow, through practice or skill or instinct, finds just the right way to reach under the wire of my bra and cup my breast just so, massage it in strong, calloused fingers, make me moan into the empty air. Sure, people could show up at any moment and catch us, but that's half the fun. My body is humming like a musical instrument, plucked into life by Ty's hands, and I can't stop the symphony.

"Never Ross," Ty scolds as he positions himself between my legs and unbuttons his pants. "Tell me, why the fuck aren't you wearing any underwear?" I close my eyes and wait for him to push into me, to take my breath away, to breathe new life into me.

"I don't like wearing underwear, you know that. Not even under scandalously short skirts." Ty makes a wicked, nasty growling noise as he frees his cock from his pants and plunges it into me. I cry out and my back arches off the platform; my hips rise to meet Ty's as he thrusts hard and fast. I think he believes he's proving a point, that we're good together, that we're *perfect* together, but I already know that. He's trying to claim my heart, steal it away from the blonde haired boy who's already lost it. What Ty doesn't know and what I should tell him is he's already claimed me, filled me up with all of him and made something new. It's as intriguing as it is terrifying, and the only way I'm going to be able to understand it is by telling him.

"Ty," I try to speak, to just get the words out, but I can't. I can't move because he is; he's moving inside of me and breaking me into pieces and putting me back together all at once. He fucks me until he comes and then he fingers my clit with his ringed hands, proving that once again, I was wrong. Boys like Ty really do know where it is and how to use it. "You're not such a bad boy after all," I breathe as he brings me closer and closer to orgasm. He laughs at this and bites the skin on my neck until it almost hurts, pulling back at just the right moment and leaving me tingling.

"I never said I was a bad boy. That was you. I'm just a man that thinks you're the shit."

"How romantic."

"I never said I was that either," Ty tells me and then he's letting go of my wrists and flipping me over, pulling my ass into the air and pushing so deep into me that I think I can feel the dark, twisted wrappings of his soul. "But I sure do love the hell out of you."

And that's just about all the talking either of us can handle as we join our bodies and souls together in the most inappropriate setting possible. Whether he knows it or not, Ty will always be my dirty, little bad boy, and that's just the way it is.

While this is happening, while I'm experiencing one of the most exciting, most invigorating moments of my life, Noah Scott stops by the house like he's done a hundred times, finds out where we've gone and hikes over to see us, bitch-Never at his side. While Ty thrusts into me, vigorous and passionate, I hear her barking in the background, but I can't see straight or even think, so I don't realize what is going on. I don't realize that my high school sweetheart, the boy I left behind, the one who still wants me but doesn't yet know that I don't want him, is standing there at the edge of the wood chips seeing everything.

From across the park, Noah Scott watches and knows that he's lost.

32

Noah Scott is sitting at my mother's kitchen table eating a bowl of cereal. He looks up at me when I come in and pause with my white robe wrapped tightly around me, my body sweetly sore from the night that Ty and I spent together. His blue eyes look into my hazel ones and I don't know what to say. *You're too late. I loved you once, could've loved you again, but Ty is my tortured, twisted other half and we're too wrapped up together to be separated now.*

I open my mouth to speak when Noah scoots his chair back across our yellow and white linoleum floor with the little chickadees on it. It creaks and makes me cringe, at the noise, at his eyes, at him coming across the room with purpose. Noah pauses in front of me with a gentle, easy smile that Ty will never have and looks at me with eyes unclouded by uncertainty and pain. He loves me, too. I can see that, but he doesn't understand me, not anymore. Noah Scott cannot understand Never Ross, no matter how hard he tries.

He puts his hands on my shoulders and leans in, nice and light, like a fluffy white cloud floating through the too-blue sky. Ty is like a rain cloud, fat and pregnant with a storm, full of crackling thunder and explosive lightning. I close my eyes and wait for it, wait for that last, perfect fairytale kiss, the one that will seal my fate and lock me away from Noah Scott forever. It never comes. He puts his lips next to my ear and whispers to me.

"Goodbye Never Ross."

When I open them, he's smiling but I think I can see the slight shimmer of tears in his eyes. Mine fill, too, and I have to look away to let him go. I have Ty now, and I can't be selfish. I can't keep Noah on the same leash forever. It's time for him to get out, to find somebody else, someone that can give him all the love he deserves without a side of crazy. Fortunately for me, I have someone that needs both.

"Morning," Ty says through a yawn, shuffling up behind me and pausing as he notices that the screen door is swinging back and forth in the morning sunshine. He doesn't say anything or ask any questions, but he does kiss me on the top of my head and move over to the table where Noah's empty cereal bowl still sits. Ty picks it up and empties it into the garbage disposal. I stare at his strong back, at the long, lean muscles and the smooth skin and I wonder how the fuck I'm going to tell him what I absolutely one hundred percent *have* to tell him.

I use the sleeve of my robe to wipe at my eyes and sit down at the table, my stomach roiling and threatening to open up on me, spill right across the perfect white top of this table.

"Good morning," Beth says as she slides in the door with a bag of groceries in either hand. Ty takes them from her before she drops them and spills bottled sweet tea across the floor. I can see it sticking up out of the bag.

"Gram would have your ass red limned and sore as a prickly pear cactus if she knew you were buying your sweet tea pre-made."

"Who's going to make it?" she asks as she ogles Ty's body and makes the hair on the back of my neck stand up straight. "You?" Beth puts the offensive beverage in the fridge and ruffles Ty's hair. "You are such a sweetheart," she tells him as he helps her unpack the groceries with an unlit cigarette dangling from his lips. Shit. Fuck. Damn. I want one so bad, my mouth is watering. But now I have to quit. Or maybe I don't? I can't possibly know until I talk to Ty about it. I can't now though, not with Beth hanging around the kitchen like a protective mother. She keeps throwing me these looks, trying to determine what Ty knows and what he doesn't know. I look away and ignore her.

The park yesterday was a failure in some ways and a success in others. A smile quirks my lips for a second and falls back into a frown. We had *the* best sex on the planet yesterday, on top of a children's play structure for God's sake, but that doesn't mean he's going to be Father of the Year. Hell, how would I even know if he was? I barely remember my dad, and I've hated him for a long time for things he didn't even do. Besides, it's not as if Ty or I have had the best mothers either. How would I know how to even be one? I can't have a baby, not now, but I also can't decide anything until Ty knows. His reaction could change everything.

I drum my nails on the table and notice that the polish is chipped. Beth sees me staring and smiles as she pours herself a glass of tea.

"Want me to get those for you?" she asks, and I can't help but smile, even through my worry, because if Beth paints my nails like she did for that last, fateful performance then I can really feel like I've come full circle, like I'm back where I started, ready to make things new again. *I'm so sorry, Noah,* I think, and I hope that after he gets over the disappointment of losing me for a second time that we can be friends. I've decided that it really isn't possible to have too many of those, even if they send you texts that say, *just fcked Trini. Was so good! Think i'm in luv,* at three in the morning. I sort of even miss Lacey and her yellow nails and perfect blonde hair.

"So," Beth begins as Ty pours two bowls of cereal and sits one down in front of me. He smiles as he slumps in a chair and scoops massive mouthfuls of Cheerios up with the pink plastic spoon that belongs to Maple. *I fucking love you, Ty.* "What's on the agenda today? Christmas shopping maybe? Oh, or we could watch some home movies?" I think for a second, really think because I need to come up with a place that Ty and I can be alone at, but where we might actually be able to get some talking done. And I have to do it fast. Every moment I wait is another betrayal, and I have to stop the clock.

"You know what," I say as I sit up and grab my own bowl. "I actually have plans. With Ty." He looks over at me but doesn't question my words. He'll call me on bullshit, sure, but something like this and he's all game. He might have a past that burns like fire and eyes that could kill with a single glance, strike right through the hearts of men and women alike, but he's all game for spontaneous. I clean my bowl out and stand up, finished even before Ty, which is a rare event for both of us. I hold out my hand, the one with the gold ring, the one that holds a perfect, blood red ruby, the one that Ty gave me and that I will never, ever let go of. "Ty," I say. "Come with me. There's someone I'd like you to meet."

33

"Ty McCabe, I'd like you to meet my father, Nicholas Andre Ross." I pause next to the old headstone and lay my fingers across the cement. My eyelids flutter closed of their own volition, and there's a second there where I'm no longer inside my own head, where I'm floating through the cemetery on the breeze, coming to rest with a sea of dead leaves, melding into the earth. Being here is so ... refreshing. I've been avoiding it since I was ten and now, I cannot believe I ever left. Despite what others may say, the dead are not frightening; they are peaceful.

I open my eyes and watch Ty in his scarf and coat. He is so *cute* like that; he makes me want to do things like *giggle* or bite my lips. I resist both in honor of my father, and try not to notice the way his hair is ruffled by the cold fingers of the wind, how his dark eyes watch my every move with interest, with love. Yesterday, he thought I was going to tell him something horrible. What, I don't know, but now, he's even more cheerful than usual, if a bit jumpy. On the drive over, he was fidgeting with his rings, spinning them around on his fingers like I've never seen him do. When he saw me watching him with a raised brow, he blurted something interesting, something that I've tucked away for later. He told me that the rings were passed down from his grandmother to his mother and that that's why he took them. Because she didn't deserve them. And then, of course, he clammed up and didn't speak another word about it. I'm getting the feeling that encouraging Ty to talk about his past is not going to be an easy thing to do.

"Nice to meet you, Mr. Ross," Ty says as he kneels down and lays a bouquet of black roses at the head of my father's grave. The flowers were his suggestion, something beautiful, something dark. *Like you,* he'd said. I smile at the memory. "I can assure you that my intentions with your daughter are in no way honorable, and I intend to ravage her quite savagely this evening." I give in and giggle which is just weird. Never Ross doesn't *giggle.* I hold out my hand for Ty and he takes it, but instead of standing up, he pulls me down and rolls us over so that his body is lying mostly atop mine.

"Tell me something," he says as he rests his head on my chest and I stroke his hair with my fingers. "If I were to, say, ask you to let me ravage you not only this evening, but everyday for the rest of our lives, how might you respond to that?"

"Sounds good to me," I respond, sighing in tune with a winter breeze. I'm taking Ty's words figuratively, but he's serious. I can see that as soon as he sits up and kneels between my legs. I've never had fantasies about fucking in a cemetery but with Ty sitting there, it's not hard to get ideas.

"I mean it, Never," Ty says as he licks his lips and shakes his head like he can't believe he's doing what he's doing. "Look, I've been alone for a long time, forever it seems, and I've met a lot of girls and I've … "

"Ty, no," I say. I don't want him to talk about that stuff, not right now. Even the thought of Ty in another person's arms, in their body, makes me sick to my stomach. He reaches out and gently places a finger over my lips.

"No, I'm going to say this," he tells me as I struggle to prop myself up on my elbows. "Fuck, Never, I have to say this before I forget how lucky I am and start to hesitate. Okay, so, you know, when it comes to relationships and friendships and all that other crap." I smile at Ty because his diplomatic speeches are always full of dirty words. Always. It's part of what makes Ty, Ty. "People like to judge them on how long they've known each other, and I just … Never, I think a real friend is someone who sees you at your worst but likes you anyway, who's there for you even if they'd rather not be." He pauses. "You're that friend for me," he tells me, eyes on the grass next to my hips and not on my face. Whatever it is that he wants to say, he's still gearing up for it, getting ready to blow my ship out of the water, my rocket out of orbit, my heart from my chest. "And … you're more than that. You're … " Ty pauses again and pulls a ring off of his finger. It's the blue one this time, the one that sparkles like the sea. "Never," he says, and then he levels his gaze on me, connecting to my inner being with just a blink of his eyes, diving in, swirling around inside of me, consuming me in the only way I want to be consumed. "Will you marry me?" Ty slips off the ring and holds it in his palm like a shining symbol of the words he's just spoken.

Holy shit.

Holy shit.

Holy fucking shit.

I struggle out from under Ty and stumble to my feet using my father's headstone for support. Ty follows after me and grabs me before I can go running, pulling me against him, his hands firmly planted on my hips, the ring digging into the flesh of my side. But then, he didn't even need to. See, I'm not into running, not anymore, I'm into guys like Ty McCabe. And guys like Ty McCabe, I guess they're into me, too.

"Are you serious?" I ask him because it's all I think to say. He nods and nibbles at his lip ring like he just can't keep still. His face is frozen, awaiting judgment. This boy, this *man,* that I picked up in a bar with no intention of ever getting to know has now just asked me one of the world's most perplexing questions. Now, I'm not a girl who's obsessed with weddings, who dreams about white dresses and tiered cakes, but I am a girl who dreams. I dream of a partner that I can split my pain with, one that understands me, that completes me, makes me whole, and now I've found him. And it's him, not me, but him, who wants to make it official, declare our love on paper, celebrate it. Ty McCabe wants me not just for now, but forever. I swallow and try to still my aching heart. It's been working so hard lately, beating for so many people, learning so many things. It's hard to keep up with it all.

I wondered once if Noah Scott could've been my knight in shining armor, but I see now that I was wrong. To be a knight, you have to save someone from something. Noah Scott couldn't have saved me from anything because there would've been nothing to be saved from. I made hard choices, wrong choices, bad choices, call them what you will, but they made Never Ross and I'm starting to see that she isn't such a bad person, that maybe she's more interesting than I thought. I see now that my knight is Ty McCabe, that he came in and helped save me from myself, and now, now I'm going to save him.

I lean over and kiss Ty on his perfect lips, feel his warm hands on my hips and decide that I won't tell him about the baby, not yet. First, I'll save Ty McCabe and then I'll tell him. I see his eyes are wide, and there's a bit of sweat on his forehead. I smile and realize that I've forgotten to answer the one question that I never thought I'd hear, especially not from Tyson McCabe, my bad boy, my tortured soul, my little piece of dark with bits of light that glimmer like stars.

"Yes," I tell him. "Yes, I will."

If you enjoyed this book, look for the third book in the Never say Never Trilogy!

About the Author

C.M. Stunich was raised under a cover of fog in the area known simply as Eureka, CA. A mysterious place, this strange, arboreal land nursed Caitlin's (yes, that's her name!) desire to write strange fiction novels about wicked monsters, magical trains, and Nemean Lions (Google it!). She currently enjoys drag queens, having too many cats, and tribal bellydance.

She can be reached at author@cmstunich.com, and loves to hear from her readers. Ms. Stunich also wrote this biography and has no idea why she decided to refer to herself in the third person.

Happy reading and carpe diem!

www.cmstunich.com

Made in the USA
Lexington, KY
11 March 2013